THE DARK LIGHT

Also by Mette Newth
The Abduction

THE DARK LIGHT

Mette Newth

Translated by Faith Ingwersen

FARRAR, STRAUS AND GIROUX

New York

Farrar, Straus and Giroux
19 Union Square West, New York 10003

Copyright © 1995 by H. Aschehoug & Co.
Translation copyright © 1998 by Faith Ingwersen
All rights reserved
Distributed in Canada by Douglas & McIntyre Ltd.
Printed in the United States of America
Designed by Judith M. Lanfredi
First published in 1995 by H. Aschehoug & Co., Norway,
as *Det mørke lyset*
First English-language edition published in 1998
by Farrar, Straus and Giroux

Library of Congress Cataloging-in-Publication Data
Newth, Mette.
    [Mørke lyset. English]
    The dark light / Mette Newth.
      p. cm.
    Summary: While enduring a bleak existence in a hospital for lepers in
Norway during the early 1800s, thirteen-year-old Tora tries to find meaning
in a life surrounded by death.
    ISBN 0-374-31701-1
    [1. Leprosy—Fiction.   2. Death—Fiction.   3. Christian life—Fiction.
4. Norway—Fiction.   5. Diseases—Fiction.]   I. Title.
PZ7.N48665Dar   1998
[Fic]—dc21   97-21484

To Hege, in memory of Tore

AMONG THE MANY kinds of illness from which humanity suffers, there is scarcely to be found any that is more cruel and painful than leprosy. The chance observer will view it in its advancing stages not without repulsion, but the more thorough observer looks at it with a tear-filled glance, the heart's deepest compassion disturbing his attentiveness; the altruist with melancholy walks away from his brother, the living-dead. And this illness—which, like the greedy worm, devours the most flourishing plant, eats its way maggotlike into the body and marks the living human being with decay's dark stamp—has just as horrible an influence on the well-being of the rest of human kind. It annuls the most beautiful relationships in human society, casts out a man from his circle of activity, tears apart friendship's most tender bonds, separates a wife from her husband, parents from their children, and makes the human being unclean, like the leper of the Orient; as a leper, the formerly pleasant, loyal, and good neighbor becomes intolerable to his peaceful neighborhood and in vain seeks in his own house the sanctuary that he is denied by law; and in church, as well as in his own house, his company becomes loathsome.

—J. E. Welhaven,
*Description of the Lepers in St. Jørgen's Hospital
in the City of Bergen, Norway*

WINGS OF LIGHT AND FIRE

1

irl, are you sleeping?"

She hesitated before she refrained from answering. She tried to lie quite still and breathe as one does when calmly sleeping. But she couldn't sleep. She feared sleep. Feared gliding helplessly over the edge of that slippery, cold precipice, down into the bottomless darkness, and perhaps never reawakening.

She wasn't certain which of the two women had asked. She didn't yet know their voices. They had said little when she came into the small room that the three of them were to share until the inconceivable happened.

But they had looked her over long and hard. Her body, her hands, and her face. She thought they did so with envy. Because she was only thirteen. Because she might still be able to resist death for a long time to come. Because she didn't yet have boils and running sores as they did. Didn't yet stink of pain and fear of death.

Perhaps they envied her the hope she clung to. The hope that it wasn't true. That she wasn't really a leper.

A leper.

The bare word shone darkly behind her eyes and overshadowed all thoughts of life. For the leper didn't belong among the living. That was what the parish pastor had said in his mild voice as the gate of St. Jørgen's Hospital closed behind her. Now she was among the living dead. Among the seventy souls that God had singled out to wait in death's outer court until it was time. Until her time on earth was up.

It was impossible to understand that she was going to die.

What had she done to deserve such a harsh punishment? Surely God didn't punish without reason?

She mustn't think about the question, for it had no answer. If she began to cry again, the women might wake up and would ask once more, *Where are you from? Do you have any family? Who is paying for you?*

Do you have any food? Will you help, you who are still young and strong enough?

She couldn't answer. Could not because of the words that burned behind her eyes: Leprosy. Pain. Death.

Suddenly her hands were wet and cold as ice. She froze as if her body were covered in frost. But it wasn't cold in the small room, for the little window was securely closed. The heat was thick and damp from the feverish women, whom she could touch without stretching out her hand.

Her straw mattress on the floor between the narrow beds was also warm, and so were the sheepskin and blanket Granny had given her. The last gift, Granny had said. It sounded almost like a judge's sentence.

The cold wasn't coming from the rain outside either. It was still late summer and the weather mild. The cold came from within her, from the ghastliness that hid within her, without her knowing why it had chosen precisely her. She knew only what it would do to her, and that she was a prisoner. Until death came.

Perhaps the hoarfrost would continue to grow until it formed a constrictingly thick layer beneath her skin. Then she would freeze to death before the illness got the upper hand. Die alone. With no way out.

Loneliness, she didn't fear. She was used to it. It was the pain that frightened her. The thought of the pain as a merciless jailer, a cold, alien being that waited crouched within her, ready to let loose a mighty punishment for the least offense.

What had she done to deserve this?

The rain drummed against the roof, and the wind rattled the loose boards in the outer walls of the great, leaky house. None of the sick in the hospital were kept awake by it. Dread and pain already kept them awake.

She stared out into the darkness. Dimly she saw the outline of the door out to the great hall. The narrow little bedrooms for the sick stood in a row, with their doors open to the hall. It was deserted, but not quiet. The whispering, whimpering voices streamed like a breeze through the darkness. They seeped out of the walls, flowed along the floor, dripped from the ceiling. Old voices, young voices, as distant as an echo and as near as her own breath:

Almighty God, deliver us from evil . . . forgive us our sins . . . have mercy on our poor tortured souls. Look in compassion on Jesus Christ's poor creatures . . .

Endless prayers edged with pain and terror.

Was God really present here? Did He hear the tortured prayers for mercy? Perhaps His ear was turned somewhere else.

She didn't know what to believe. But she dared not think that God did not exist.

Then all hope would be lost.

The parish pastor had said that there was but one recourse to be found—salvation. She had to surrender herself to God. Surrender herself and endure until He received her, for she was one of His chosen. God chastened those He loved the most; He had given His only begotten son for mankind's deliverance. It was all in the Holy Book, the pastor had said. That Book which she herself could not read.

When the pastor preached in church about God's love, she had felt herself to be weightless at the promise of salvation. That was before. When God was as mild and distant as rays of sun in the mysterious darkness. When Jesus on the cross was a bone-white wooden doll with rust-red stripes of painted blood on its breast and loins; when she wished only to assuage the pain in that cracked face.

That was before she herself needed solace.

Before she needed to approach God.

When the parish pastor said that the illness was a sign that she was chosen and that He expected something from her, God had drawn closer. Like a threatening cloud in the sky, she had thought. But she could not surrender herself to Him, for she did not understand His will, and she could not comprehend why the election had to be so cruel. Would He hear her prayers for mercy? Would He answer the question that tortured her most: Was she rejected or elected?

Could anyone answer that?

A black shadow glided past her door, stopped, and filled the doorway with a deeper darkness than the dark itself. She felt her eyes widen and her heart pound. Had He heard her? Had He sent the ferryman already?

But the shadow in the doorway was silent and immobile, and she stared until her eyes grew as dry as sand. As afraid to see as not to see what was hiding in the darkness. As afraid of sudden death as of seeing the dying. Those with faces disfigured by boils, without noses or mouths, with eyes coated by thick yellow film.

Here, behind the locked gates of the hospital, they didn't need to cover themselves as they had to in the town of Bergen.

When she had stood alone before them in that sun-white yard, she had stared and stared and known that she would never forget the naked, the loathsome. She had looked for a way out, but the buildings lay in a closed square around the yard, and she could not turn her eyes away from the dark bundles that sat, lay, and stood close together, staring at her. Whether they were children, men, or women she did not notice. She saw, as in a mirror, only her own terrifying fate.

But I am not like you! For my skin is still soft and my body supple, and my eyes are clear. I can still escape, for the spots from the illness can be hidden.

She had said none of this out loud. But the oppressive silence before her spoke just the same.

You are not the first who has refused to recognize her fate and has wanted to flee. We were like you, and you will be like us.

No one had approached her.

She neither dared nor wanted to approach them.

She had crept by them, walked in a big arc toward the entrance to the great hall of the hospital. But she could not avoid their knowing glances. Ashamed and angry, she had huddled in the darkness behind the entry door to the hall. There she sat, immobile, with her knees pulled up and her arms around her little bundle of clothing. Her fingers clutched the wreath of flowers that her sister had woven for her. It still gave out the sweet, wild fragrance of the distant fields at home, though the flowers had long since withered.

So she sat and held on tight to the diminishing fragrance of a sun-warm meadow of flowers on the steep side of a valley, until two elderly women came to fetch her to evening prayers. Without a word they brought her into the hospital's church. Just as silently, they sat down on either side of her in the pew.

She had seen shapeless shadows quietly moving up toward the altar railing and for a short moment a few faces in the flickering light from the two nearly burned out candles on the altar. Beyond the circle of light the darkness was filled with dragging steps and whispered prayers for mercy and absolution. Like thin smoke from a dying fire, the prayers rose toward the high roofbeams.

She clasped her hands and mumbled in whispers like the others. But she prayed no prayers. She felt no remorse, no surrender. Just anger. A hard lump of unanswered questions.

What do You want with me?

Why me?

Wasn't it enough with Mother?

"Pride is a great sin." This was softly mumbled beside her, and she quickly turned her head. Both women sat with bowed heads, deep in prayer. After that she no longer dared to think, just mumbled along.

The evening light disappeared, and the darkness thickened behind the large windows that, high up in the wall, faced on life outside the hospital. A woman and a child walked by chatting. Then came the loud cursing of a man who was dragging an all too heavy load.

She mustn't wonder how they looked and where they were going. Not remember the injustice. Not ask whether punishment on earth was necessary to being rewarded in heaven.

The two women had accompanied her back to the bundle and the wreath, which still lay behind the entry door. After that, they took her along to the little room that they were to share. There was just enough space for her mattress on the floor between the beds.

The women had begun to question her. At first they were cautious, then more insistent. That sudden closeness made her panicky, and she did not dare open her mouth, afraid of screaming out her aversion, afraid of vomiting from the smell of terror.

They had turned away. As if she had struck them.

The dark shadow continued to fill the doorway. Just as immobile, dense, and silent as before. She felt nothing from it. Neither menace nor assurance. Just an expectant silence. What was it waiting for?

That she should beg for forgiveness? That she should admit that there was no way out, no place to escape to? Or was it waiting for her to recognize that no mercy was to be found without surrender?

Suddenly she felt the cold abyss beneath her. Felt anew how her numb fingers vainly clawed for a hold on the slick rim of ice above the waiting chasm, and she heard her silent scream, while the sun's disk blinded her eyes, which could not be closed.

Again a cool shadow fell across her face, and she saw, spread out, mighty wings of dark light. On their outermost edges could be seen a fine rim of white fire, and the voice said, *You shall not yield before you have to.*

That luminous edge of flame had not been there in her dream before.

Slowly the slippery abyss again became a dry mattress, and the heat of the women's bodies closed about her. The blue vault of heaven melted into the darkness of the hall and an empty doorway. The slight outline of outspread wings glimmered in the darkness. She sobbed with relief and something that resembled happiness.

Her fall toward the chasm had been stopped. By mighty wings of light and fire and a voice she longed for all too sorely.

hat was only a dark speck against the sun's disk before, slowly gliding toward them, grew until its outspread wings covered the sun and its head, with the powerful beak, and its claws, ready to grasp its prey, were very near, and the eagle had looked calmly at them until, with mighty beats of its wings, it flew into the sun and then, with its wings enveloped by the sun's fire, plummeted to the ground.

Tora and Endre heard the sound of something heavy and soft striking stone.

They looked at each other. Uncertain. They had neither heard nor seen that the eagle had been hit. They had scarcely recognized that it was an eagle before it was right above them. But Tora remembered its glance. The eagle had looked at them calmly, without curiosity, without fear, before it flew into death.

They sat a moment and listened.

They heard the roaring of the rapids below them and the wind that played among the leaves of the birch trees. Faintly, they heard the sheep bleating in the spring pasture. But from the mountain's edge it was quiet. Completely quiet.

"A golden eagle," said Endre breathlessly, and dropped the pruning knife and the load of newly cut birch branches. "Come. We must see it."

"Maybe it's not dead," she said. "Then it is dangerous, it could attack . . ."

"Eagles don't lure people to them by falling from the sky! Eagles hunt and catch only what they need, that's all."

"But I know they attack people when they are threatened."

"This eagle is dead, Tora. We saw it plunge, we heard it hit the mountain. It did not live through the fall. Listen!"

From the edge above them there was absolute silence.

"I have never seen a golden eagle at such close range before," said Endre. "Don't you want to see it, too?"

He could not hide his disappointment.

She did not answer. Just continued to wipe the leaf sap off the pruning knife in her lap. The spicy fragrance made her nose itch.

He squatted down before her. "Are you afraid, Tora? I can go alone; then I'll bring you its finest tail feathers."

"Of course I'm not afraid! You know that."

Her anger confused him. She hadn't been like that before, so quick to misunderstand him and defend herself. Something was wrong that she would not talk about.

They had collected foliage all day: climbed up and down the gnarled birch trunks, cut the branches with the thickest clumps of leaves, taken care that enough remained for new growth. It was strenuous work.

Tora was the smaller and lighter, so she had climbed the most. She had long felt the pain dully throbbing in her legs. For many days past. Now it was like a toothache. She did not have the strength to climb up the slope of loose stones to the mountain edge.

"It aches," she mumbled apologetically. "There."

She pointed.

Her legs were thin and slightly rosy, with slender ankles and straight toes. Winter cold and summer dampness had colored her toes deep red, for she went barefoot in all kinds of weather most of the year. Only in winter did she use stockings and clogs.

Endre squeezed and pinched her legs.

"Hmm," he said, as if he knew what he was doing. "I can't feel anything. That surely doesn't hurt either?"

"No."

She almost laughed at his solemn demeanor.

"Not here either?"

He pressed hard against the swollen spots on the insides

of her legs. The spots had appeared after a bad fall onto a pile of stones down below the hay barn.

She shook her head. "I don't feel anything there," she said. "I don't even feel you pinching, Endre. But it aches. Inside my legs. That's the only reason I won't climb up to the eagle. I can't."

"Then we'll wait," answered Endre.

He got up. "The eagle won't fly away. It will be here when we come up again."

"But a wolf could take it," she objected. "You go, Endre."

"But I want us to see it together. You remember our secret? Or have you outgrown it?"

Tora shook her head.

He glanced up at the sky. "Anyway, it's time to start for home with the fodder for the sheep."

Endre went first down the steep, twisting path, carrying both loads of foliage. She followed behind with the pruning knives, through a green mist of tiny showering leaves. The farms, the strips of hayfields, and the small patches of tilled fields lay far beneath them, nearly invisible in the fine spring rain that had begun to fall as soon as they had gotten up to go.

All she saw of Endre under the loads of leaves was the light tuft of hair that always stuck obstinately up in the air and his strong, bare legs, which stepped with such certainty between gnarled roots and sharp stones. He whistled, and now and then he talked, loudly and cheerfully, but his words were lost in the rustling of the foliage on his back.

He wanted to cheer her up, she knew. To try to help her to think of something other than the aching. He was like that.

They had known each other forever.

They had grown up together on the two farms cleaving tightly to the mountain where it arched its back before diving down into the ice-green fjord. The farms lay in a circle around a farmyard that was a common workplace and playground for Tora's and Endre's families. Around the farmhouses lay green specks of cultivated and outlying fields. The narrow mountain ridge was otherwise bare, except for belts of twisted birch forest across the outlying fields.

Their families owned equal parts of the small strips of fields, but they worked them together. The joint effort provided more hands to share in the labor and greater strength against long, hard winters. The joint effort also provided safer care of sheep and goats in the mountains, since the children from both farms tended them together.

It's best to be many when you live far from other people, said the adults. Both Endre and Tora knew that it was true. But they also knew that there wasn't one big flock of children, as the grown-ups believed. There were two flocks on the farms, each with its absolute ruler: Tora's big brother Mons and Endre's big brother Erik. They were the same age, were equally strong, and found the same enjoyment in bullying others. And what pleased them was usually detrimental to Tora and Endre.

Tora and Endre were the same age and the youngest in each flock of brothers and sisters. They had both been chased home when the larger children had something secret going that "the babies" couldn't take part in. Never had Endre tormented Tora as her brothers did when they themselves were harassed. Endre and Tora had found consolation together by leaping across the stones in the dangerous rapids. In spring, when water thundered wildly off the mountain. In winter, when rough black-green sheets of ice held the rapids captive. Never had they mentioned that daring game to anyone. That their friendship was unbreakable was something they had discovered one late-summer day in the year they both turned seven years old.

The whole of that scorchingly hot day, black banks of clouds had been building up above the mountains. As the thunderclaps increased in strength, the adults and children from both farms toiled to get the hay into the barn before the oppressive heat was replaced by lashing rain, which could continue for a long time. The day was an endless stream of loads of dry hay on bent backs down steep slopes from the field strips, of angry shouts and slaps from the grown-ups, of horseflies and burning sun. Then it ended of course with a fierce fight between Endre's older brothers.

"That's enough!" his mother had shouted, so it had rung across the hayfields. "Get down to the hay barn, all of you, and be quiet! It's almost suppertime!"

Cheering, Mons and Erik had led their flocks on a mad dash toward the cool darkness of the hay barn. It was while they were lying in the fragrant hay that Mons had asked who would dare to jump down from the barn roof.

Silence descended while everyone thought about the distance from the slick old slate roof to the nettle thicket far below.

It is high and dangerous and difficult, Tora thought, and saw before her, below the hay barn, the steep pile of rocks with the lush thicket of nettles filled with old rubbish and sharp stones. But she said nothing. Not even when Mons began to brag about how often he had jumped.

But, as Tora knew, that was in winter, when snowdrifts cushioned the blow of sharp stones and rubbish. No one had dared the jump in summer, as Mons well knew. What was he up to now? Tora had tried to make herself invisible behind Marit's back, but Mons examined his brothers and sisters with a piercing look.

"Now others will have to risk it," said Mons, and smiled at Erik. "Or are there only weaklings in your family?"

"Not at all," answered Erik just as calmly, "but, like you, I have jumped enough for a while. But my youngest brother, Endre there, is quite a brave fellow. And, I know, likes to fly. He doesn't do much more than gather feathers and play bird. He'll jump for us."

The thunderclaps sounded much nearer.

"I won't do it," said Endre.

"Of course you will, you sparrow!"

Erik's voice was sharp and his mouth tight-lipped as he got up. He was much older than Endre, long-legged and broad-shouldered.

"I won't do it," said Endre, his voice still low. He said no more, did not try to escape. Just sat calmly refusing to give in to his big brother towering above him.

It was as if Tora saw him properly for the first time. Slight and stubborn and alone in a slanting beam of sunlight that made his bristling hair shine as white as flour.

"You will," snarled Erik. "You'll do what I want you to!"

Tora held her breath. Between Erik's legs she met Endre's glance. She saw no fear. Just a kind of tiredness.

"You can go jump yourself," said Endre. He nearly smiled when the resounding box on his ear came. "I won't do it."

"Don't you have any discipline in your flock?" Mons laughed scornfully and got up. It was then that Tora had shouted, "Don't do it! Leave him alone!" and Mons had turned his gaze on her and said slowly, "Well well, there are others here who want to fly," and before she knew it, she was standing beside Endre and being tied up with a rope as well.

It was not a game. It was deadly serious. It was about who made the decisions in the flock. Everyone knew who that was.

Tora's and Endre's eyes met again, and Tora saw that he was thinking, Anyway, they won't be able to make me cry.

Not me either, she answered mutely, and let herself be lifted up on Mons's shoulder without kicking or screaming. Like two lambs ready for the slaughter, they were transported to the roof by Mons and Erik and placed astraddle the outermost part of the gable.

"You two can either sit here till the snow comes or jump," snarled Erik. "The rest of us are going to eat supper."

Then they left, the rulers and their subjects, and Tora and Endre were alone on the roof, with thunderclouds swelling ever faster out across the sky.

They were quickly rid of the rope. Their disgrace was something worse. They couldn't just cast it off.

"Are you afraid?" Endre turned and looked at her.

She shook her head. She had been most frightened when she understood that she had to defend Endre. Now she was mainly angry.

"Is it true that you like to fly?" she asked carefully. That, he had never told her.

"I've collected a lot of first-rate feathers and bird bones

on the mountain," he answered quickly. "You can look at them sometime."

"Sure, but do you really pretend to be a bird?" She didn't give up so easily.

Even though he turned his head away again, she saw that he was blushing. His ears, which stuck out beneath his bristly hair, were fiery red.

"Have you decided to take root here, or are you going to jump?" he asked gruffly.

She thought about it. She wouldn't call for help. If she did, she would certainly get twice as bad a beating from Mons. She wouldn't climb down. It was less dangerous than jumping, but the shame would be unbearable.

"Actually, it's quite nice sitting here, don't you think?" said Endre. "You can see so far, straight to the home of the trolls."

She understood that he wanted her to think of something other than jumping and the thicket of nettles far beneath them.

She nodded and swallowed. Her hands were strangely cold.

The black clouds covered the whole sky now, and the peals of thunder came closer.

"I'm jumping. I don't feel like waiting until I drown," said Endre almost indifferently. He had stood up and was balancing far out on the edge. "Anyway, I've wanted to fly from the roof for quite a while. Watch me the next time it booms, Tora. Then I'll fly like a thunderbird!"

"But . . ."

Tora stopped short. Of course. He wanted to jump. He had wanted to the whole time. He just wouldn't be forced.

"I will, too," she lied. When he smiled, she was suddenly happy about the lie. "As long as we don't . . . kill ourselves?"

"You must make believe that you're a bird," he said eagerly, and immediately reddened, as if he had revealed a great secret.

"You must believe that you can't fall, because you were created to fly. You know that the air will support you if you only use your wings as you've learned to. They're strong and supple; you can sail or rise, dive or brake with your wings. Your tail feathers know how they're supposed to steer, and your legs know how you're to touch down on the ground . . ."

Tora was completely overwhelmed. It sounded almost like magic.

"Which bird do you most want to be?" he continued. "Close your eyes and think hard. Don't be afraid. I'll jump first and catch you."

The next clap of thunder made the hay barn shake. Then he jumped. She saw him float for a moment, made luminous by the lightning, a thin figure with arms like outspread wings, blindingly white against the black sky.

She shut her eyes tightly and tried to feel like a swallow, a bird with a little light body and long, narrow wings. But it was difficult to think of anything other than doubt. What if the force of magic didn't work? Then she would fall to earth like a stone. It was perhaps madness to believe Endre, but defeat was worse.

She heard him hit the ground and tumble about in the undergrowth. But he groaned only once, no matter how much it must have hurt.

"Get up and jump far out, quickly!" he shouted. "Tell me which bird you are!"

"A swallow," she stammered, and got shakily to her feet.

"No, swallows fly too low in storms, Tora! You're a hawk flying high and free, with powerful, broad wings you can safely rest on, in all kinds of wind! Do you hear? A hawk!"

"I'm a hawk!" she shouted, and jumped, and in that brief moment before she hit the ground with a painful jolt, she experienced a wonderful feeling of freedom and weightlessness.

He caught her and protected her with his body against the sharpest stones. They floundered around in that stinging underbrush for a long time before they got out of it.

Then the rain came, violently, and they hurried into the hay barn. They sat in the warm hay behind the latticework of rain and examined each other's injuries. Injuries that they had received because each in some way had tried to protect the other.

"You are my best friend," said Endre quietly.

"You are my best and only friend," answered Tora seriously.

They spoke no more of friendship, but they agreed that they would never again yield to their big brothers.

The bruises and cuts disappeared when summer was past, but their triumph over their big brothers lasted a long time. Their friendship they knew would last forever.

In summer as in winter, Tora and Endre met at the mountain precipice above the gnarled birch woods and watched the birds hunting and playing, mastering their wings and the winds. The two never grew tired of seeing how the ravens caught the lemming or of speculating on why the snowy owl and the ptarmigan changed into their winter plumage. Was it God who decided that they should have a white feather coat in winter, or did the birds themselves know that white on white was the best protection? In that case, how could the birds determine that they would change their plumage?

As the years passed and they opened up the world for each other, Tora and Endre grew closer.

What was odd was that the secret they shared, which at first had been a game and an escape from bothersome sisters and brothers, had now become the most important thing to them both. The secret bound them together. But it also separated them from the other children. No one else cared to, or had the patience to, lie still for hours to follow the buzzard's gliding across the sky. No one else would dream of discussing how the buzzard could know precisely when it should dive dizzyingly toward the fjord to catch its prey. No one else wondered whether it was God who determined when each bird should fall to the field or if the birds determined it themselves.

The golden eagle they seldom saw. It was always as distant as God.

Never had they seen it so close as on that day when it flew against the sun and plunged into the mountain.

3

everal days passed before they could get up on the mountain again.

Tora and Endre were at an age when they no longer could get away whenever it pleased them. They had to work both early and late like all the others. After the hard winter there was an excess of chores on the farms. The big brothers, who had not forgotten Tora and Endre's rebelliousness, were careful to divide the tasks so that the two of them always received an ample share. It was often the heaviest and most unpleasant toil that fell to them. To gather foliage in the birch woods was something the brothers knew they both wanted to do. Consequently, there would be a long spell between the occasions when they received permission to go up to the woods.

Tora felt the pain throbbing dully all the time now, and it happened more and more often that her legs gave way beneath her. Even though the paralysis never lasted long, it frightened her. But today the spring wind was so strong that it nearly carried her up the steep trail to the twisted birches.

"We'll look for the eagle first," she said, before Endre managed to ask if she had the strength. Then she continued up to the knoll without turning around.

It lay outermost on the mountain knoll with its wings stretched out and its head bent backward in a tautly drawn bow. The eagle looked as if it were still flying, long after death. No predator had been near it. It lay there exactly as it had fallen.

"What made it fall?" she whispered, almost afraid that the powerful bird might come back to life.

"Maybe it was sick or old. Maybe it knew that its time was up. So it might just as well fly straight to God," answered Endre. He bent over the eagle without taking notice of the buzzing flies and the sweetish stench of rotting flesh.

"Do you really believe that it decided on its own death?"

He nodded. "The parish pastor would probably not like all that I believe and know about animals," he said cheerfully. "But, then, he won't get to know about it either, will he?"

She shook her head.

Endre grabbed one wing and pulled it. The wing came loose easily from the body, and he lifted it up toward the sun's white disk. Beneath the powerful, dark feathers shone strong, narrow bones with a pink glow.

Beautifully alive even though the bird was dead.

"See, that's how things really are, Tora. Dead and ugly outside, but still beautiful inside."

They sat for a long time admiring the eagle wing. The supple bones were still easy to move beneath their feathered dress, which rustled dryly in the spring wind. Tora managed to forget the stench and the flies and the throbbing pain in her feet.

"You should have wings"—he smiled—"since your feet hurt so much now."

She turned her head away. She had thought the same thing, of course! But their carefree bird game was over, no matter how much they tried to hold on to it.

Endre plucked the finest feathers from the wings and tail and laid them in two equal piles. Tora plucked out the softest down from the bird's breast. Granny would make a lovely pillow out of it. That ought to soften her up.

Tora did not immediately discover that Endre was sitting quietly staring at his hands.

"You can have all the feathers, Tora," he said suddenly, and shoved his pile over to her. "I'll keep just one."

"Why don't you want to keep them yourself?"

"You must have them. As a remembrance."

"As a remembrance? Why?"

"Because I'll be going away."

"Going away? Where?"

It was only then that he managed to tell her what his father had decided for him. Endre was to travel to Bergen and take a job as a hired hand for a merchant who was in the dried-fish trade at the wharf—Bryggen. Endre was fortunate to have been offered work and to be able to earn money, his father had said. There were too many of them on the farm now, and Endre, who was the youngest and soon a grown man, had to get out and support himself. Erik, who now ran the farm together with his father, thought so, too.

They listened for a long time to the roar of the rapids, while each avoided looking at the other. Far, far down below lay the farmyard with the farmhouses where someone had determined that they should be parted. They saw the aerial cable for transporting hay and wood. It was just a little thicker than a hair when viewed from up here. It ran from the farms down to the boathouses by the fjord, which glittered white where the sun shone on the water and smoldered blackish-green in the shadow of the mountain on the other side.

"Will you row there?" asked Tora. She could think of nothing else to say.

"No, I'll walk across the mountain. It won't take many days."

Silence descended again.

All she wanted was to say something that would make him less unhappy. Something that would diminish the pain of parting, but she could not think of anything other than the very worst.

"Bergen is far away. Maybe I'll never see you again."

"We'll see each other again, Tora."

He turned and looked at her. "For we belong together. You know that now. Don't you?"

She nodded. Yes, she knew, even if they had never said so to each other. She seldom imagined herself as a grown-up, as a married woman with her own children and her own life. But when she thought about her life as an adult, Endre was always there. It was impossible to imagine a day without Endre.

"I'll work hard. I'll save money. I can find work for you, if you want. Maybe as a servant girl for some wealthy tradesman?"

She smiled quickly and nodded.

Kind Endre. She would not let him leave feeling worried about her.

"In a year I'll fetch you," he said firmly. "Then we can be together the way we want to be."

"The way we have to be," she said softly. "I'll wait for you. Always."

Tora knew that it sounded like a pact for life. "If you can't come to get me, I'll go to Bergen."

"Do you promise?"

Tora nodded. She didn't dare look at him again. She had never before seen him cry.

She stared up at the sun and saw a great shadow gliding toward them, for a moment translucent before it became the dark outline of a golden eagle resting on its wings as it hung right above them, and then again became one with the sun.

It must be his mate, thought Tora. Even in death.

There was a strange consolation in that.

Endre had not had time to come for her. Before the year was out, Tora was in Bergen.

But she did not walk across the mountain as Endre had. She was driven in the parish pastor's wagon, for her feet could not support her that far.

Even if Tora was grateful that the pastor drove her, she also knew that it was not merely an act of kindness. He wanted to be certain that she left before she spread leprosy to more people on the farms cleaving so tightly to the mountain ridge. For even if the pastor never said so, Tora knew that he was thinking of her mother. He had not gotten her away in time. Nor had he managed to prevent her from choosing her own escape from leprosy.

Tora thought of her mother without cease. But she did not think of the contagion or the sorrow, only of the madness and joy and a wonderful milk-white wing with sky above and below it. On the whole long, bumpy road to Bergen she thought of her mother. When the gates of the hospital were closed behind her and they said that now she was dead to all the living, Tora could think only of deliverance.

4

t was one of those rare autumn days when everything was almost transparently visible.

Far out on the horizon, the enormous pale-blue sky rose above the snowy mountains and the plateau, afire in red and green. Never that Tora could remember had the mountain lake been so bright, and never had the roseate clouds mirrored themselves so clearly. Never had she felt so light and free. Never had she seen her mother so carefree.

Her mother had awakened Tora early that morning, whispering, "Come, we're going up into the mountains."

Tora had looked at her sleepily.

"Hurry up! Be quiet. This day is yours and mine and no one else's."

Tora climbed carefully over her sisters and brothers, who were still asleep in the large bed in the loft of the smokehouse.

"I want to show you something beautiful, my sweet," her mother said when Tora questioned her.

They had taken along fishing lines and berry pails, but they let the fish swim undisturbed in the mountain lake and the cloudberries glow in peace on the bogs. For a long time they wandered side by side, listening to the wind that shook the bog cotton and reeds, the ptarmigan that hurried through the scrub willow, the bees that buzzed in the heather.

It was a day when the air tasted sweet and sharp from a surfeit of summer. A day Tora knew that she would always remember, not only because it was exceptionally beautiful, but also because she had her mother all to herself, for the first time in a very long time.

They rested on the shore of a large lake, on a flat slab of rock covered with golden moss.

A wild goose glided toward them, broad-breasted and commanding, with a flock of half-grown youngsters in a tidy wedge formation behind it. The goose lay by some way from the shore and started to crop the rushes with loud smacking sounds. Tora smiled. She could almost taste the juicy reeds between her teeth. She knew exactly how the mother goose dipped, cut the tough stocks with her sharp beak, threw her long neck backward, and swallowed, dipped, cut, and swallowed. Again and again, while she vigilantly took care that her young cropped the reeds exactly as she did.

"She is preparing them to manage by themselves," said her mother quietly. "That is every mother's duty." Her voice shook.

Tora glanced quickly at her mother. Her face was nearly hidden beneath a profusion of billowing hair. Its red-gold color Tora proudly recognized as identical to that of her own.

Lately her mother had refrained from wearing a matron's headscarf and had begun to let her hair hang loose, as only unmarried girls did. "I want to feel the wind in my hair," she merely answered whenever anyone asked. "Surely it can't hurt, since we live so far from other people."

Granny had snapped her mouth closed, and Tora knew she thought that it was just like that wild daughter-in-law of hers to defy all demands of pious decency.

After that, her mother had stopped accompanying her father when he played for a wedding or a party on the farms along the fjord. Tora had not understood why her mother would no longer go with him, but she knew that Granny was quite pleased by it. Granny had always believed that fiddle playing was the devil's work and that it was not at all suitable for a married woman to run around to the farms of strangers and make a show of herself. Granny's mouth became as thin as a blade of grass when Father called Mother "dance-happy Ranveig" and bragged that her singing could move a stone to tears.

"Perhaps we had better start home now." Her mother sat up.

Tora felt her mother's sudden melancholy like a cold gust of wind.

"But this is our day, isn't it, Mother? The sun still hasn't reached the midpoint of the sky, and look, the wild reindeer are running across the glacier!" She pointed. "I want to go closer, don't you?"

"Of course," answered her mother in high spirits. "But it's far, Tora. Can you manage?"

"Of course. I could go to the ends of the earth with you." Tora laughed. She bent over and pulled her mother up.

They stood for a long time with their arms around each other without saying anything. Tora felt her heart beat and her breath draw in, in the same rhythm as her mother's, and suddenly their bodies were one, as they had been when her mother's milk and warmth were the only things that kept her alive.

"You are my sweetest one," her mother whispered down into Tora's hair. "The precious apple of my eye. You whom death nearly took away from me. Come, we have much of our day left before sunset, and maybe we'll see the Magic Reindeer."

"The Magic Reindeer?" Tora gasped. She had to trot to catch up with her mother, who suddenly began to stride on.

Her mother told her about the Magic Reindeer, the oldest and wisest of all reindeer, which leaped from mountain peak to mountain peak on moonlit nights and guided the herd when the winter storm lashed the earth and the sky white.

"No hunter can get it in his sights," finished her mother. "It is too shy of people. But it surely knows that we don't want to harm it."

I wonder if it's true, thought Tora as she leaped behind her mother from grass clump to grass clump in the bog, a glittering carpet of deep pools up to the edge of the glacier. She was panting and soaked up to her waist, but it didn't matter, not even if the Magic Reindeer was only a fairy tale. The day with her mother was wonderful anyway.

High up on the blue glacier stood nearly a hundred reindeer sharply silhouetted against the sky. The animals had seen them and waited, uncertain whether the danger was so great that they would have to start bounding over the ice ridge.

"Be quiet as a mouse," whispered her mother. "Maybe they'll dare to trust us. I want so much to see them up close."

"Can you call them to you?"

"No! The animals are wild. They can't be fooled by a call. But we can try to charm them closer. They will perhaps come if we wish it fervently enough."

They lay quite still for a very long time. The sun burned their backs, and their stomachs were cold. Beneath the hard, thin crust of the glacier the snow was dry and as fine as powder.

It was not at all unpleasant to lie on, thought Tora, when for a moment she let go of her fervent wish that the reindeer herd should come closer.

Then she saw a movement ripple through the herd, and a white doe leap out.

She was slight and beautiful, with a milk-white coat and large coal-black eyes. She remained standing quietly for a moment before she suddenly trotted in a large circle in front of the herd. Then she came toward them, calmly.

Tora and her mother lay immobile and stared as the doe slowly drew closer. Her black hooves broke through the ice crust with a crisp crunching sound. Her eyes did not leave Tora's mother. Without hesitating, the doe continued until she stood right before them. Then she bent forward, sniffed thoroughly but carefully at Tora's mother's face, and stared into her eyes. For a long time.

Tora saw the rosy, soft muzzle; the large, nearly transparent ears, covered with hair as fine as down; and the deep black eyes, with equally thick black lashes. She had never seen a more beautiful animal. Tora was overwhelmed by sudden happiness and awe.

It was impossible to know what was going on between the doe and Tora's mother just then, but their eyes locked for a long time. Tora scarcely dared breathe.

Suddenly the doe tossed her head.

It was as if she was done with something. She stared

past them, at a point neither of them could see. Then she spun around and galloped up toward the waiting herd. As if on a signal, they formed a long line behind her, and she led them in a grand ring dance, prancing in steadily growing circles across the glittering glacier, until the snow spray from their hooves covered the faces of Tora and her mother with a fine, cold powder and the animals' soft snorting filled their ears.

Then, all at once, the herd was transformed into a mighty spearhead that rushed behind its milk-white leader toward the glacier's crest.

Tora and her mother lay silent until the herd had completely disappeared, then they rolled around in each other's arms. Around and around in the dry snow, while their laughter and tears blended together and neither of them knew who was more of a child.

"Was that the Magic Reindeer?" gasped Tora.

"Who knows? In any case, Tora, she gave us a magnificent moment," said her mother quietly.

She lay on her back staring up at the sky.

Tora crept up close and pressed her nose into the soft hollow of her mother's throat. "I want to be like you," she sniffled.

"You *are* like me, my sweet. Don't you know that? And I'll never leave you," whispered her mother. "Do you hear? I'll always be with you. Even when you can't hug me to pieces as you are doing now."

She got up. "Come, the sun is going down; we must start for home."

"Do you want to know a secret?" asked Tora when they had put the bog behind them.

"Gladly."

Her mother listened attentively while Tora told about Endre and the birds and the dangerous game at the rapids and about the day when the two of them flew from the ridge of the roof.

"But there is something more, isn't there?" said her mother.

Tora nodded. She had never thought that she would tell her mother about the domineering big brothers, about the all-too-obedient flock of brothers and sisters, and about its being impossible to bow to the brothers' will.

"So that was how Endre and you became friends." Her mother laughed. "I wondered about it. Don't think that I'm blind to Mons's greediness for power," she continued, suddenly serious. "But unfortunately no one can teach you to have the courage to live your own life, not even your own mother. You must find courage within yourself and the strength to keep it up. It takes time and it is lonely work. But it is worth all the effort, for you will be free, and you will be in full and complete possession of yourself. You must just never give up. Never yield. Never surrender before you see that that is your last resort."

She took Tora's head between her hands. Her eyes were

misty when she continued: "I only wish that I could say this more clearly, Tora, but I do not have the words. Just believe me when I say that you might have to fight to live your own life, and you'll then need great courage, a courage that almost seems like madness. Remember that."

Tora nodded. She wanted to cry, but she held back her tears. The moment was too solemn. She knew that her mother was telling her something enormously important, even if Tora didn't understand why.

Before they began the steep descent to the farms, they stopped on the meadow in front of the little summer dairying cabin. They sat there, enjoying the last rosy light of evening. Tora knew of no finer view. The mountain crests resembled a white rim around the edge of a huge greenish-gray bowl, with the fjord a blue splash at the bottom. From up here the farms were no larger than nutshells, but their sounds reached them anyway, thin and clear over the roar of the rapids and the bleating of the goats that climbed around on the steep slopes just below the dairy cabin.

"Come here, come here," Mother called softly, and listened.

The bleating stopped.

"I wonder if they'll come," said she.

"I know of one that will surely come." Tora smiled.

Sure enough, immediately afterward they saw her coming, a large and shaggy, grizzled animal, too old and heavy to bound about like a kid. But bound she did, until she was right up by Tora's mother and could lay her head against the mother's shoulder. She bleated loudly and offendedly and pressed her round stomach with her milk-heavied udder against Tora's mother's leg.

"Oh, you don't say? Has no one bothered to milk you today? That's not surprising. But now I'll give you some relief so you can leap about on the mountain with those big kids of yours."

"She becomes like a kitten when she sees you," said Tora.

It was always to her mother that the animals came, with stones in their hooves or a kid that refused to eat. It was always her mother who found the nanny goats that had gone astray or gotten stuck on a mountain shelf. It was she whom they trustingly followed when slaughtering time came.

"We've something in common, you know, we who are mothers." Bent over the goat's back, Tora's mother laughed. The berry pail was half full of rich milk.

"I've always turned to the animals," said she, and straightened up. "Ever since I was a little girl. When I was alone with them at the dairy cabin for the whole summer, I enjoyed myself the most. There's more goodness to be found in animals than in human beings. They're not malicious, judgmental, or vindictive. They accept life as it is. They simply live life until it ends. Peacefully and simply. Not like some people I know who'll do anything at all here on earth to obtain eternal life."

"Who is it you're thinking about?"

"I won't talk about it now," she said fiercely. "It would only ruin the rest of our fine day. You'll no doubt find out when you've grown up a bit more."

Tora looked at her dejectedly. Again the door to the adult world had been shut.

"There you are; now you're rid of your burden."

Tora's mother straightened her back and smiled at the goat. It rubbed against her affectionately before it began to bound down the steep slopes.

Tora's mother turned toward her. "Now I'll show you something truly beautiful."

She lifted the pail and hurled the milk.

It flew out in a broad stream. For a moment it remained above them, hanging motionless, before it was dispersed into falling drops. In that wonderful instant Tora clearly saw a wing, pervaded by light and floating freely with a golden-red sky above and below it.

Tora heard herself gasp.

Her mother turned to her and laughed, that warm laughter that always made Tora so tremendously happy, even when she didn't understand what her mother was saying or doing.

"It's like a miracle, isn't it?"

Tora smiled carefully and waited for an explanation.

"Ugh, that look of yours. It reminds me frightfully of Granny's!"

Her mother laughed delightedly. "If she had seen that,

she would have ranted and raved about sin and folly. Granny doesn't know what joy or delight is. She has never allowed herself either one, for fear of God's punishment. Watch out, Tora, for people like Granny. The self-righteous who in God's name smother all joy in life."

She squatted down before Tora. Her eyes glittered.

"Did you see the angel's wing of gold?"

"Yes, I saw it." Tora smiled. "Thank you."

"I wanted so much to give you one more beautiful moment to remember from this day, which has been ours alone. Nature has been so generous to me. Now it was time to show how greatly I celebrate it. Promise me that you'll remember this."

She took Tora in her arms. "My dearest, I wish so fervently that you always will have the courage to experience those moments in life that are so beautiful that pain nearly surpasses joy. Promise me that you will always dare to follow your heart's desire whenever you can!"

Tora at once felt uneasy. Not because she didn't understand everything that her mother said, but because her mother spoke so sincerely, as if it was necessary to get everything said right now.

Her mother stroked her cheek. "You are yourself a child of my heart's desire. I have loved you more than any other. In you I see myself as I once was."

She stopped. Her voice was teasing when she continued: "And I know about your love for Endre."

Tora started and blushed violently.

"No, no one else knows about it."

Her mother's face was suddenly close by hers, and Tora saw the large brown spots on her mother's forehead clearly for the first time. That terrible change which she had hidden so well beneath her flowing hair.

Suddenly Tora felt the day turn around and its happiness disappear.

She wanted to scream, but her mother held Tora tightly to her.

"Hush now, my most precious. Things are as they are. Just promise me to keep up your courage. One day you will need it in order to choose to be completely free."

A short time afterward Tora's mother vanished.

She had said that she would look after the goats, and she had not wanted anyone to accompany her. Not even Tora. When evening came and her mother had not returned, Tora could no longer bear her anxiety. She begged Mons to go out with her to search, but he thought there was no danger, since their mother was strong and at home in the mountains. Besides, it was too busy on the farm for him to leave right then. Their going could wait until their father came back. After all, he was supposed to come at any moment.

Tora got no help from anyone. She did not bother to talk to Granny. She knew exactly what Granny would say about Tora's irresponsible mother.

The days passed without any sign of life from her mother.

Tora ached with premonitions of the very worst.

Her father did not come back early from the settlements along the fjord as he had promised. As he always promised and never did.

At last Mons also became anxious and decided that all the children should go searching in the mountains. The whole time Tora knew where they would find their mother. She had known it ever since the day her mother disappeared.

Tora crossed the bog first.

It was covered with a thin film of ice.

The air had suddenly grown colder.

Tora did not see her at once, for she lay in a spongy hollow nearly covered by a quilt of powdery snow, with her arms stretched out and her face turned to the side. Like a reddish-golden halo her beautiful hair lay spread about her head. It was covered by a fine veil of frost that made her look like a young bride.

She lay as if she had fallen from the sky.

The tracks of a hundred dancing reindeer formed a large ring around her.

Tora felt a sudden intense joy for her mother. A joy so great that it was difficult to distinguish from pain.

It was here that her mother had wanted to leave life.

She had chosen the glacier with its enormous open sky as her final resting place. It was here she wanted to be for all eternity. Not beneath the heavy clay of the graveyard by the narrow fjord, buried under a small, bare, wooden cross.

When Tora's loss became too painful, she went to her mother's resting place on the glacier. She often saw the reindeer herd trotting across the glacier, but the milk-white doe was never with them.

It never came back.

5

omething had awakened her, but she didn't know what. A movement, a shadow past her eyes; a cold draft, as from a door suddenly opened; a sound, a dry crunching like small stones underfoot. She didn't know what it was, because she had been in the dream in which her departure was always different from what it had actually been.

In her dream it was always quietly raining. Drops as light as the very first snowflakes fell and fell against the face in the casket on the way to the graveyard under the open sky.

In the dream Tora was always the one who felt the wagon stop with a jerk, who heard the men catch their breath before they carried the coffin up the slope, who heard the silence in the graveyard as hands were clasped in prayer for the poor sinful soul who had taken her own life.

In the dream, clumps of wet sod fell thick and hard. Fell and fell until the body became the earth it had come from, and the earth-black darkness was splintered by blinding light, and everything became nothing.

But it had been her mother who lay in the narrow casket with her hands folded over blooming heather. Tora had walked behind the casket beside her father, who didn't dare play her mother into heaven, where she belonged. Tora had walked as if blind, without being able to distinguish the rain from her tears, which ran and ran.

It was not the dream that had awakened her.

Something was present here when she woke up. In that little room where the stench from the sores of the women in the beds on either side made her nauseous. The women slept with their faces turned toward the wall and with blankets that moved in the same quiet rhythm as their breathing in sleep.

Something had been here. It was not here now.

She saw the doorway. A pale-white frame around the still, gray light of the hall. The trees outside the little room's window sketched sharp patterns of twigs and leaves on the wall around the door. Tora stretched her arms toward the light and saw the shadows dance darkly across the large spots of her illness. For a moment she remembered a meadow with the heads of flowers swaying in the summer night. But they were not flowers luminous with life that she saw on her arms. She saw bleak omens of death. Nothing could change that.

Quickly she covered up her arms.

She waited until her breath grew calm again. Not until then did she have the courage to throw the sheepskin coverlet off and begin the elaborate, daily investigation of her calves and toes.

In the beginning, when she had first understood that the spots did not disappear by themselves, that they were not marks from falls or from Granny's hard pinches, she had avoided looking at them. She hoped that if she just did not notice them, they would disappear. But they were not to be exorcised in any way. They only became larger and more numerous.

She didn't remember exactly when she had forced herself to examine them carefully for the first time. But that was the day that terror came. It came quietly and clearly and filled her with the certainty that she would die. Then, finally, she understood that the spots lived their own life and had their own mysterious reason to grow and spread across her skin. And she knew that the illness would transform her into an old woman. A repulsive, crippled outcast.

That, her mother had escaped.

That, she herself would have escaped if only she had dared.

Now she at least managed to examine the spots. Thoroughly, without trying to lie to herself. Always with hope and fear in attendance.

The spots had not become smaller since yesterday. Neither had they been suddenly transformed into open abscesses. That time would come, of course. The moment when that would happen, she feared the very most.

She didn't stop until she had investigated every tiny part of her body. No, neither had the leprosy come sneaking in this past night to stamp her skin with new signs of doom.

Luckily.

Luckily? What was so lucky about leprosy coming on slowly?

Death was certain anyway.

She mustn't cry now. Just survive. Minute by minute. Step by step, into the unknown.

She concentrated on controlling the pain.

It was stronger and more insistent today.

It was impossible to know where the pain came from. It was just there, deep within her. An aching that ran through her body like an underground river. Without beginning. But with a definite end.

She gasped.

Someone had been in the room and had sneaked away.

She thought of the shadow in the doorway the night before. That was something else.

Quickly she scrambled down to the end of the mattress

and fumbled for her bundle. It was not lying where she had hidden it. She found it nearly beyond the mattress. It was lighter than she remembered. The knot was untied.

Someone had been in the room. Someone had opened her bundle. Someone had taken the bread and the smoked mutton bone and the money that the parish pastor had given her to pay the director of the hospital. Someone had taken everything she needed to look after herself.

What was she to do? What would they say?

She shook with fear.

The parish pastor had repeated over and over again that she had to take good care of the money. The food, too, she had to take good care of, and be chary with, for privation was great at the hospital. It was all the fault of the great war, he had said. The great war was far, far away, in a distant part of Europe. But it brought misfortune and misery to Norway. Therefore, the hospital was poor.

It was impossible to understand. Tora knew nothing about the great war. Just that it was here at the hospital. Together with death.

"What are you thinking about, girl?"

The voice was whisperingly close, and the hand on her arm was warm and chapped.

Tora stared up into the woman's friendly face. It was lined, but without boils or sores.

"Pull on your skirt and follow me," the woman continued. "But be quiet. It's a good thing that these poor creatures are sleeping, so they are spared hunger for the time being. They probably don't have much time left."

Tora dressed, grabbed her bundle, and followed the woman through the dim hall with the long tables and benches and out to the kitchen, where there was a fire on the hearth under a gigantic iron pot.

"I'm Marthe, the night nurse. Who are you?"

Tora opened her mouth. She wanted to answer obediently. But the words did not come. They had turned to stone.

"You don't need to answer yet. Sit down on the bench, so that you can have a little soup to drink. Actually, you patients are to prepare the food yourselves, but I'm afraid many would succumb all too quickly if I didn't cook a little soup once in a while. Most of it is water, and the least of it is food, unfortunately, but it still warms you."

The figure before the steaming kettle on the hearth was large, broad, and friendly like the voice and face. She chatted without stop, but she seemed to be listening while she spoke.

"As a matter of fact, I know who you are, Tora Monsdatter Tveiten. I've heard your father play many a time. No one could play like he could, and no one could dance like your poor mother."

She stopped abruptly and stirred the pot briskly. As if she checked herself from saying too much, thought Tora, but she didn't have the strength to ask what the woman knew.

"We're nearly from the same settlement, you and I," continued Marthe immediately; "I'll bet you didn't know that. I was born at Skar, innermost in the fjord. But it's been . . . since I left home . . . Oh well, it's been a long time. More years than I care to remember."

The steaming bowl was in front of Tora. She lifted it with stiff fingers and slurped carefully. The soup burned her tongue, but it felt good to have a sharp pain that came from the outside.

"I . . ." she began. Then she became mute again.

The back of Marthe, the night nurse, was listening in the same friendly way as before.

"It's hard in the beginning, before you get used to being one of the outcast."

Marthe paused a moment. "But after a while you'll understand that everyone here is like you. Different and special. It's only the leprosy that makes them alike. You know, there are all kinds of people here. Farmers and fishermen, peddlers and townspeople, poor people and well-to-do people."

The voice was confidentially close to Tora's ear. "Wait until you meet Mistress Dybendal. You've never seen the like, so fine and pompous. But mysterious and extremely difficult to deal with. Many here are afraid of her, and she keeps to herself in her little room on the second floor. Sometimes you can see her when she is wandering in the gallery in the dark, back and forth, almost like a caged animal. She has awful pains, that I know."

As she spoke, Marthe's fingers raced across Tora. Light, warm fingers that investigated Tora's scalp, forehead, jaw, and throat.

Tora sat quietly and let it happen. But when the fingers neared her arms, she jerked and squeezed her bundle hard against her breast.

"I'm not going to hurt you, girl! I just have to find out how far along you are. You surely understand that I must!"

She stared at Tora with a wrinkle between her kindly eyes.

Tora tried to smile while she squeezed the bundle tighter.

"What is the matter, can't you tell me about it?"

"I . . ." began Tora weakly. Then suddenly the words came in a tear-edged shout: "My food and money have been stolen! What will you people do with me?"

"That, too, poor child, as if you didn't have enough trouble!"

Marthe rocked her gently in her arms. "How can you understand what is happening to you? Go ahead and cry; you need to, for it's beyond understanding. I really am so very sorry."

Her arms held Tora tight and safe while Tora cried and listened to her voice.

"You do not know . . ." whispered Tora finally.

"Oh yes, I know all right. I've lost everyone myself. The

sea took my husband and four sons. Leprosy took my daughter, my very dearest. But God spared me, and I am His servant here for as long as He decrees it."

She smiled and stroked Tora's hair. "Perhaps we'll be here equally long, you and I, for you should know that leprosy is not equally hard on everyone. You can live a long time, if God so wills. If you keep up your courage."

If God so wills. But she had not surrendered herself to God.

Perhaps this was the punishment.

Perhaps He was sitting in His high heaven right now, waiting for her to be frightened enough to surrender herself.

Tora drew her breath, trembling.

"Don't be afraid. You'll manage all right."

Gently Marthe lifted Tora's face and dried her tears.

Obediently Tora sat quiet, with her eyes closed, while Marthe examined arms, hands, calves, and toes.

"You're lucky, Tora. You'll keep the use of your hands and feet for a long time."

It sounded like a mild sentence.

Marthe went back to the pot and stirred for a long while. She looked grim when she continued: "It's a crying shame that people at the hospital steal from one another! Haven't we enough misery already? But it seems that poverty brings out the worst in people, doesn't it?"

Tora was not at all certain Marthe was talking to her.

"This town and its citizens were generous to the hospital's poor children of Christ when times were good, when there was enough work and food. But unfortunately kindheartedness tends to vanish when times grow hard. The good pastor nearly wears himself out going around begging for funds for the patients. He speaks to and writes to and pleads with the government officials for money, but they turn a deaf ear to him. Had it not been for goodhearted seamen, who now and then give a couple of bushels of rye or a barrel of herring, the poor creatures here would have died of hunger long before leprosy took them."

Tora tried to follow it all carefully, but she managed neither to hear nor to understand what Marthe said. All that she could think about was that her money was gone. The money that the hospital had to have for her care.

"The parish pastor said that I had to . . ." she began.

"I know."

Marthe's voice sounded tired, nearly impatient.

"You were to take good care of the money that your county had to pay the hospital on your behalf. But now it's gone, and I'm certainly not going around turning over the mattresses of the miserable wretches here. Let me take a look inside your bundle so that I can truthfully say to the superintendent that we have made a thorough search."

Tora handed her the bundle and watched while Marthe shook first the stockings, then the blouse. Four large eagle feathers floated to the earthen floor. Some bread crumbs lay in the flowered scarf. Marthe replaced everything nicely.

"No money here," she said.

"It was in the embroidered purse I got from Mother."

Tora swallowed. "I got it the winter before she died. It's so beautiful."

"We'll probably find the purse one day." Marthe's mouth was a thin line. "But it's best to forget the money."

"What shall I do without money, tell me that!"

"Cry no more about it, Tora. There is always a way out. At the very least, I'll see to it that everyone shares in the little bit we receive. I'll talk to the superintendent. You can pay for your keep by working. There are many here who can no longer manage on their own, but you are still young and strong. You'll be free of debt, and the sickest will get the help they need. Isn't that indeed right and reasonable?"

She looked at Tora sharply.

Tora blushed. Ashamed, she remembered the evening before, when the women had asked about the same thing. Meekly, as if they expected her to say no. Then she had drawn away from them. Without pity. Now she needed their sympathy.

"Yes, it is right and reasonable. Besides, I would like to help."

At once she knew that she meant it, as frightened as she was.

"Show me what to do."

"That I will."

Marthe smiled, but she looked stern when she continued: "But first you must learn to conduct yourself like decent people do. Come around with me and greet the others properly. Show the sick respect, Tora. They deserve it. They are suffering enough without being treated like outcasts by other sick people. This is your family now, whether you like it or not."

6

ever had she experienced anything more oppressive than the walk around the hospital. Her shame was the worst. Worse than the pain.

Slowly she went from one person to another, curtsied low, and mumbled her name.

They received her as if they had been expecting her. All of those who had dragged themselves up and were sitting on the benches in the great hall, those who still lay in their little rooms after a sleepless night, and those who would never again rise from their beds.

She forced herself to stand still, while her heart beat in wild flight, and some asked where she came from, some touched her, and others begged, weeping, for her help. She answered faces that were gaping holes without mouths or noses. She stared into pale-yellow, blind eyes. She held fingerless hands that reached out to her. And the whole time she knew that she would always remember each woman and man, each child and each old person that she met on this first day in hell on earth.

She wanted to beg for mercy, but Marthe's rigid back spoke volumes: *You cannot escape becoming one of them. You must make your peace with this life of yours.*

Wasn't that exactly what they had silently said to her in the hospital yard the day before? Then she had desperately told herself that the illness could be kept at a distance, if only she didn't go near them. Now she had admitted the truth, and all protection was gone. Maybe death would come more quickly now that she was one of them.

The thought was almost too much to bear.

She staggered after Marthe over to the stairs to the second floor.

Nausea had become a sour lump of phlegm in her mouth. Her heart beat with hollow, irregular throbs. She clung to the railing and pulled her leaden body upward. Step by step. Her head was amazingly light atop her heavy body. And filled with a swirling wind that drove her thoughts around and around, like dry leaves.

She stopped to check her dizziness.

She looked down.

In the hall far below her she was met with stares.

Was it sympathy or recognition she saw in their eyes? Had they all loathed themselves and each other just as intensely as she did?

The gallery was dark and narrow and went around the entire second floor. On one side lay the little rooms for the ill. On the opposite side was the fragile railing above the great hall. The darkness was broken by squares of light from the open bedroom doors. Just one door was closed.

"We'll go there last," whispered Marthe. "That is Mistress Dybendal's room."

Tora nodded. She could just barely hear Marthe's voice above the rushing of the wind in her own head.

The walk on the second floor, like the walk on the first, was unbearable.

The same bare rooms with tattered mattresses on narrow beds. The same worn clothing and blankets with strange patterns in the dark colors of dried blood and infection. The same exhausted, rasping breathing, as from ruined bellows. The same pools of mucus and excrement in cracked wooden bowls and vessels. The same sweetish stench of suffering and coming death.

It was enough.

She didn't want to feel more loathing. She no longer had the strength to feel ashamed. She wanted to sleep.

Tora stopped.

"Come, there is only Mistress Dybendal left."

Marthe tried to smile. She knocked hard on the closed door.

Tora waited. For Marthe's sake, she would try. But her body had become snailishly slow and moving was painful.

Something strange was happening to her without her wanting, or being able, to do anything about it. The wind in her head had increased in strength, and someplace, far behind the wind, a cry sounded. It was still too far away for her to be able to grasp its meaning, but she heard that its tone was triumphant. She felt surprisingly happy, almost excited. It was as if someone were trying to help her.

But there was, of course, no salvation to be found!

Marthe again knocked hard.

No one answered.

Marthe opened the door and shoved Tora inside.

"You have a visitor, Mistress Dybendal. Our new patient, Tora Monsdatter, would like to say hello."

Marthe's voice was respectful but reproving when she continued: "It is polite to answer."

The woman sat on a chair by the window. Its back was turned toward them.

At first Tora saw only the chair. She had never before seen such a beautiful chair. It had exquisite carving, a high back, and curved legs. But its costly leather upholstery was worn and cracked.

Marthe cleared her throat. She waited impatiently.

Mistress Dybendal didn't move.

Tora didn't pay attention to either of them. She looked around.

The room was the same size as the others at the hospital, but it was not equally bare and wretched. A little slender-legged table stood beside the chair. On the table was a tall candlestick on a large black book with silver mountings.

Tora guessed that it was the Bible. A book like it lay in the church at home.

The candle must have dripped for a long time. Mistress Dybendal had obviously not bothered to stop it. The congealed pool of tallow on the Bible was large and had run down onto the fine lace tablecloth. There, the tallow had formed an equally large pool.

In the half-dark corner by the window, she glimpsed a big-bellied pitcher and a roomy basin. It looked as if the blue flowers on the basin were growing up from the red washwater.

One long wall was entirely filled by a large travel chest. It was beautifully painted and had fine fittings. On the lid of the chest lay a long cape, which flowed toward the floor in black waves of velvet, a denser black than that of darkness itself.

With icy clarity, Tora knew where she had seen it before, and she hurriedly turned her glance to the bed.

It was narrow, like all the beds at the hospital. But the bed linen testified to Mistress Dybendal's high birth. There were warm blankets, a pillow, and a linen sheet. Covering the bed was a fine white woolen throw, embroidered with an incomparably beautiful garden, full of flowers and birds and wondrous animals in rose, yellow, blue, and green. Once that beautiful garden had been bright and clean. Now it was marred by large rusty red and dark yellow spots.

Leprosy spared neither the wealthy nor the poor.

The figure on the chair suddenly rose without turning around.

Her back was straight and her waist small, and her thick hair flamed reddish-gold in the sharp sunlight.

Tora gasped. Only one person in the world had hair like that, but she rested under the earth with heather in her hands.

"What are you gaping at?"

The voice was light, but the tone was snarling. Like a savage dog's.

"Now, Mistress Dybendal . . ." Marthe began, and laid her hands protectively on Tora's shoulders.

"I have told you to leave me alone! Will you never stop these foolish visits! I don't want to see your pathetic poor. Do you understand that?"

Tora felt Marthe's fingers tighten with anger, but her voice was calm when she answered, "Your arrogance will someday cost you dearly. I promise you that. Then may God look upon you with mercy."

"What mercy? Where is God in this house of tortures? What else awaits one here but death! No thanks, old woman. I'll manage without His mercy!"

She nearly spit out the words. Her straight back quivered.

"Quick! We must get out before she does something worse!" Marthe's fingers had become claws in Tora's shoulders.

But the Mistress had already turned and slowly strode toward them.

"Look at me well, girl, and understand that you are looking at your own fate! Then tell me if you believe this is the work of a merciful God."

It was too late for Tora to close her eyes to that terrible sight. Beneath her red hair, her face was narrow, where its shape was still visible under the boils. Her skin, which was that of a young woman, was dark brown and as lined and wrinkled as an old leather shoe. Where her nose should have been was an open sore with a flash of the white tips of bone. Only her eyes were undamaged, blue-gray and clear, but filled with a rage so burning that it scorched Tora.

"Here, wench, you shall have a present from me!"

And she threw something so quickly that Tora didn't manage to shield herself from it. She caught it, and suddenly the Mistress's forefinger, as dry and gnarled as the bark of a dead tree, lay in her own hand.

"You monster!" gasped Marthe.

Death seized hold of Tora and pulled her to itself in a dizzying embrace—in a grip that she knew would never again be loosened.

Without Marthe, Tora would have swooned.

Without Marthe, Tora would not have had the strength to get out and away from the wild breakers of the woman's desperate anger.

"Now do you understand, wench?"

The woman's shout thundered in Tora's ears long after the door had closed.

To be sure, Tora had understood. But she didn't understand how she was going to endure the rest of her short, pain-filled life here. She wanted to go far away, to a place with a clean, high sky above a blue-glimmering mountain. To the white doe's steady glance and her mother's frozen calm.

In her head the shout sounded suddenly, clearly:

> *You shall not endure this!*
> *Run toward the light, toward freedom!*
> *Use your wings, now. Now!*
> And she ran
> down that fragile bridge of light and darkness
> and hurled herself toward the blinding light.
> There was cracking
> a loud, tinkling sound,
> but her fall through the tall window was stopped.

"No!" shrieked Marthe. "You must not! You don't have the right to give up! Do you hear?" She shook Tora like a rag doll. Shook her and cried while she pulled Tora down the stairs, through the hall, and out into the courtyard.

In the sun-shimmering autumn air Tora hung in Marthe's arms and vomited until her stomach felt clean and empty and only cramps were coming in bitterly sour thrusts.

"Poor child, you are more sick from fear than you are from leprosy. Forgive me. I should have spared you, for I know how devilish she can be. God knows what drives her. I just hope it will soon be over."

Marthe stroked and stroked Tora's hair, but Tora scarcely listened to her. She stared at the slimy puddle on the ground. Large and milky white, with bits of undigested grain, it reminded her of something. A creature with pointed wings dipped in dark blood.

Her mother used to read signs in water and milk. She could decipher signs of what was going to happen to people and to animals. What could she have read in the puddle from Tora's stomach? She didn't know, but all at once she felt relieved and calm.

Her head was empty and quiet.

The wind, the enticing wind, had quieted.

"I will bury the Mistress's finger," she said aloud.

Marthe stared at her open-mouthed.

"I will. Evil must be buried."

Marthe said nothing. She just looked terribly tired and old. She remained standing quietly while Tora went into the hall.

Tora nodded kindly to those who were sitting at the tables eating.

She went up the stairs and found the finger where she had dropped it outside the door of the Mistress's bedroom. She lifted it up carefully.

It was no longer threatening. It lay in her hand like a little dead animal. Beneath the dry flesh she saw the small white bones. Beautiful life, even in death.

Tora buried it in the courtyard. She marked the place with a little cross made of two sticks tied together. Just as she had done so many times at home when kittens died.

"Rest in peace," she whispered quickly.

It was perhaps the only peace the Mistress would experience.

7

t was raining.

The rain poured down steadily the whole fall and winter, interrupted only by days with thunderstorms or biting wind.

Tora listened to the drumming on the roof of the hospital. Would it never end? The rain pushed its way in everywhere and made the walls and floor shine wetly. She felt the cold dampness through and through, and the pains pounded more intensely than ever in her body, arms, and feet.

The endless rain had caused great damage. In the church it seeped in through innumerable cracks in the roof and formed large puddles in front of the altar and on the pews. Night and day Tora heard the dripping from the church roof, a ghostly carillon that called her to God's house to try to keep it dry.

In the barn the two cows bawled unhappily. They were

starving in stalls filled with stinking water and mildewed hay. The rotten roof of the barn had collapsed during the violent storm that had raged for many days before the last downpour began. There was no one to repair the roof. No one. Tora and the night nurses, Marthe and Rannveig, had enough to do routing the water away from the muddy courtyard, water that threatened every day to flood the hospital and the church. Tora dreaded having to go out.

She strove for a long time to open the door from the hospital to the courtyard. The wind struggled against her. She didn't want to go out into the breakers of icy rain either.

She remained standing in the doorway.

Behind the mist that drifted endlessly down from the dark mountains, she saw that the peaks continued to wear white cowls of snow. The wind had the sharp scent of late winter. The sky was leaden gray and swollen with rain. Winter was far from over.

She felt a terrible dread. Not just of going out in the lashing rain, but of going out at all. For the first time, she was to go beyond the hospital's gate. For the first time, she was to stand face-to-face with the healthy's fear of the leprous. All at once the hospital seemed to her like a sanctuary and the town like a prison.

There is no way around it, she told herself sternly. She had to. She was one of the few who could. There was no more food at the hospital. Neither was there wood for the stoves, nor medicine for the most ill, but those had to wait,

Marthe had said. Food was the most important. Perhaps the Benefactor knew what to do about the other things. He could work wonders.

Marthe always just called him the Benefactor—the lepers' friend and Good Samaritan—that large man with the mild glance and the calm voice who was the pastor and doctor and superintendent of the hospital. She maintained that he could get even the most hardhearted citizen to listen to his prayers and to contribute a mite for the support of the poor inmates of the hospital. The Benefactor saw everything and heard everything and had a word of consolation for all, said Marthe. But his mild glance turned to steel and his calm voice could shake with anger when he spoke of the conditions for the lepers at the hospital.

Tora had heard and seen him. She listened devoutly when he preached God's word in church, and she curtsied respectfully when he came on his busy visits to the very sickest. But she had not talked to him, even though she had been at the hospital for half a year now.

"Take heart. You'll get to talk to him soon enough. But you don't need him now as sorely as many of the others do," said Marthe severely. "This is the worst autumn and winter I can remember in all my time here at the hospital. Never has there been such bad weather, so little money for food and medicine, and never so many dead. I can't remember the Benefactor's ever having to fight so hard and speak so urgently about compassion. He manages to soften some citizens with his prayers, but the authorities in

Bergen do not allow themselves to be moved so easily. Not even the Benefactor can make the deaf hear. That poor man is burning his candle at both ends on behalf of all of you. Mark my words!"

Tora had felt guilty. Here that good man was, wearing himself out for them, and she, who still retained the use of her limbs, refused to go into the town to try to obtain food.

Leprosy had spread more slowly in her than in many of the others. To be sure, the spots had long since become bluish, swollen sores with yellow flowers of pain at their centers, but she could still manage to walk, and she could use her hands without pain that was all too great. For that, she was thankful. Both day and night during the last weeks she had had to sew shrouds for the corpses.

Tora knew nothing about the authorities in Bergen, and she dared not ask. Sometime later Marthe would surely tell her about them when Marthe was not so desperate over the ravages of death or so exhausted from work and night vigils.

That all this had to do with the great war, Tora knew, but she didn't understand how it all fit together. She understood that it was the authorities in Bergen who determined how much money the sick at the hospital should receive each day. Marthe had explained that the value of money had fallen so low that the sick could not manage on the same amount that they had received before the great war. The sick were starving and the hospital was disintegrating. But the authorities in Bergen refused to understand that when every cent was worth less, the sick had to have more pennies. One had to trust in God and the Swedish king, Marthe had sighed at last. Then she had bade Tora to go down to the fish wharf to try to sell the clogs that Johannes had made before he died. Tora was to buy food with the money.

She had begged beseechingly not to have to go. Marthe knew, after all, the dreadful stories the others told about what could happen out there among the healthy. Tora could not bear to encounter that. Didn't Marthe understand?

Marthe was silent.

It was while Tora was preparing Johannes for the funeral that she changed her mind. While she was holding the emaciated body of a man who weighed scarcely more than a year-old lamb and striving to close his mouth, which in death still gaped for air, she had decided to venture out after food. Before they all died.

None of the other sick people had enough strength. Fever and tuberculosis ravaged just as mercilessly within the hospital as the storm ravaged outside it.

Marthe had smiled in relief when Tora said she would go. She brought her big black woolen shawl and put it around Tora's shoulders.

"There now," she had said, and bundled the shawl carefully around Tora's head. "Just keep your face hidden in the shawl, then no one can guess that you are a leper. It scarcely shows."

"Shouldn't I . . ." Tora began and stopped. She didn't have the strength to say it.

"Of course you ought to carry a bell or shout a warning. But we cannot risk your being chased home empty-handed. Not when so many here are suffering so cruelly. You just go without giving warning, and may God forgive me for concealing the truth this one time. He'll surely do so," she concluded hopefully.

Tora drew the shawl more closely around the left side of her face. The leprosy showed there the most. She picked up the heavy basket with the clogs.

"If you don't get anything sold in this beastly weather, try to beg for some herring. Fresh would be best, since salted herring is not good for the most ill. Go to the peasant fishermen from the islands north and west of Bergen; they are usually in high spirits when the spring herring have arrived."

Then Marthe had shoved Tora toward the door, before she herself ran back to the hall and the long-drawn-out howl of yet another dying patient.

Tora started down the stairs. The muddy water already covered the highest step. It would run across the threshold before she came back, but there was nothing she could do about it. The most important thing now was food.

The water reached above her ankles. Her skirt was immediately soaked and clung heavily to her legs. She had to struggle to make her way over to the gate that opened onto Markegate, Division Street. The cold crept up her legs and ran down from her shoulders. A chilling cold that numbed her pains but did not dampen her terror. Her teeth chattered and her hands shook while she fumbled with the gate's heavy lock.

She couldn't remember how things looked outside. The day she had come here, from her past life, she had lain mute and still in the back of the pastor's cart. She had scarcely paid heed to the town, which she saw for the very first time. She had not noticed its wealth of color and luxuriance or its labyrinth of crooked streets and narrow lanes, impenetrable passages and dark byways. She had not noticed the common people's houses bunched closely around steep courtyards, Dutch-style private houses that strutted behind broad market squares, stately houses that climbed up across the sharply sloping mountainsides, or the innumerable church spires that pointed up to the promised paradise.

Tora opened the gate toward town. A town that shut her in and cast her out. A town where, after leprosy had attacked two more citizens, fear and loathing for the leprous now burned as high as a fever.

The long, cobblestone-paved Division Street stretched out before her, with its rows of workshops and houses on either side. Never had she seen such a peculiar sight. Never so many people either.

It was frightening. She wanted to turn around, to flee back, but the gate slammed closed behind her and she could not turn around. She did not have the right to. She

75

had to be brave. Had to go on. No one else could. They were depending on her.

She pressed against the gate and tried to make herself invisible.

The dizziness would surely abate soon, so that she could begin to walk. Calmly and naturally. No staggering or falling; then they could discover her and all would be ruined.

No one noticed her.

They were all going about their own business. The smith and his apprentices in the smithy hammering red-hot iron in a cloud of steam, the basketmaker discussing prices with two wet and angry old women, the men pulling overloaded sleds and handcarts down the mud-slippery street, youngsters chasing hens and dogs between the legs of the adults.

They didn't see her, the wives and girls with heavy baskets, who chatted, shivering, down Division Street, didn't see that she sneaked after them across the large square, Torgallmenningen, down toward the fish wharf.

They knew nothing of her fear of being unmasked by them. Or of her longing to be one of them, a girl with fresh, ruddy skin, one who was not waiting for death.

Tora stopped. She gasped.

The town that spread out before her was frightening, foreign, and wonderfully beautiful. She saw the houses that climbed up across the steep mountainsides and the fish wharf, which teemed with people and stands and sales counters. She saw Vågen, the mighty harbor, gray and foam-lashed by the wind and with a welter of crossing cargo craft, sailing ships, rowboats, and vessels. She saw the rows of warehouses and wharfside sheds on both sides of Vågen, so close to the water that it looked as if one could row into their rooms.

There was a deafening noise of voices hawking and shouting orders, swearing and clowning, scolding and singing. A merry shout drowned out everything else:

"The herring is here! Spring herring! Big herring! Big Winter herring! Come and buy! Don't wait!"

She was gripped by the intense happiness and expectation that surrounded her, and for a moment she forgot herself completely. She wanted to hug and clap, dance and shout with joy, haggle and scold. She wanted to be alive and free, as they were!

Suddenly she remembered who she was. Dread seized her.

How was she going to manage, to be both invisible and simultaneously visible to those who wanted to buy a pair of fine clogs? How should she venture forth, she who was too shy to talk to strangers, who had always hidden behind the barn at home when the musicians came to fetch her father to a party or a peddler mistakenly wandered up to the farms on the mountain ridge?

She stared enviously at the women with their baskets

filled with penny buns and bread. Shouting confidently, they hawked their wares, poked and pushed, pulled on jacket sleeves and shawls, and stuck the tempting, warm bakery goods right up under people's noses, so that they could not avoid buying.

All at once she felt hunger like a smarting pain inside her mouth.

She *had* to manage to sell the clogs. She was going to buy fish, of course. But perhaps there would be money enough for a loaf of bread in addition. She had not tasted fresh bread in such a long time.

She looked around eagerly for possible customers.

Who could one imagine buying clogs here?

Not the men in the black coats who pushed brusquely past her. Or the women clad in capes of the most expensive English cloth, those who stood close together in intimate conversation and looked as if they owned half the wharf. Nor the pale, thin woman with bare feet who begged her way through the crowd with a flock of youngsters in tow, or the clowns with drums and tambourines and leather boots on their feet.

But farthest out on the wharf she might be more lucky. There, the peasant fishermen, farmers, and sailors stood shoulder to shoulder. There, a brisk trade was going on from brimful cargo boats with slapping sails. There, she would probably find someone who needed clogs.

She just had to try.

Tora drew a deep breath and called, "Clogs! Fine clogs! Come and buy!"

But the shout drowned in the loud buzz of voices that spoke foreign languages and dialects she did not know.

She had to go even closer to the edge of the wharf.

She pressed and nudged all she could, and suddenly she was standing right before a merry, red-cheeked fisherman. Then she screamed at the top of her lungs: "Clogs! Fine clogs!"

"How much do you want for them?"

The question came as a surprise. She had almost given up hope of catching anyone's ear.

"Can't you answer, wench?"

The fisherman who asked was a huge, husky fellow with a red face and a thick white beard, streaked brown from tobacco.

"I think . . . a couple, ten pennies?"

She could hear how stupid it sounded that she was uncertain about the price. Why hadn't Marthe thought of that! Or why hadn't she herself, for that matter?

She saw that he was suspicious.

"Do they cost ten pennies or not?"

She hurried to say that that was the right price.

"That's way too much. They're not worth more than seven," he grumbled. "A shame, since I need five pair for my crew."

He turned his broad back on her and was about to go.

"Wait!" called Tora in panic. He mustn't go, he who was going to buy everything she had all at the same time! "You can have them for seven pennies a pair."

He turned slowly around and laughed scornfully: "You aren't much of a saleswoman! If it is so easy to haggle over your price, I might as well try a bit more. Seven is also too much. Remember that I'll take them all."

All at once Tora grew terribly afraid.

This was dangerous! she was quite certain now. She was playing a game she didn't know, and she had made a mistake. That was easy to see. But she couldn't imagine how she could make up for it. How she could complete the deal and come away with the money.

"Please, good man, be merciful. Give me enough that I can buy herring for my sick and hungry family," she implored ingratiatingly.

The fisherman's pale-gray eyes turned cunning. "If that is the way it is, wench, we can just as well make a trade. You'll get the herring from me, and I'll get the clogs from you. Follow me."

Without waiting for her, he forced his way past the crowd at the wharf's edge and jumped down into a cargo boat, which pitched heavily and uneasily in the waves. The huge fish tubs were filled to bursting with glistening herring.

"Hand me your basket, so we can make an even trade," said he.

Tora bent forward.

Just a little longer now and everything would be all right. She would come back to the hospital with food for everyone. The herring could stretch into enough meals for several days, if only Marthe made the fish soup thin enough. She herself might get to taste fresh bread another time. Tora's stomach knotted with hunger at the thought.

The fisherman had taken her basket with him, past the overly full tubs with their shiny, fat, fresh herring and into the hindmost part of the little cargo boat's stern. She saw that he was poking around in a dirty wooden container. Suddenly she grew anxious.

"It must be fresh herring," she called. "The sick can't tolerate salt . . ." She could have bitten her tongue when she saw his look.

"What kind of sick people are they that they can't tolerate salted herring?" he said slowly.

Tora saw that the basket was still empty.

"There are so many frail toddlers with weak stomachs," she lied. "Please, give me fresh herring."

"You'll get both kinds," he decided. "Salt herring is good enough for fishermen's youngsters. Then it's certainly good enough, I'm sure, for the youngsters of mountain farmers!"

Tora didn't dare to say more. She would just have to be grateful that the basket would be full.

He came stomping back and stretched the basket out toward her. She eagerly bent forward to receive it.

"By the way, where do you come from, since salted herring doesn't agree with you?"

"From Voss," she hurriedly said.

She grasped the basket with both hands and pulled it toward her. But he held it back.

"And how shall you get back there with fresh fish if I might ask?" He laughed derisively.

She didn't dare answer but continued to pull with all her might.

At that moment there came a violent gust of wind. It caused the boat to rock hard and the fisherman to let go. But by then he had already seen her face beneath the shawl, which the wind had seized.

She saw, rather than heard, his shout: "A leper! For shame! Wench, you're a leper!"

She wanted to hurry away, disappear in the noisy crowd.

But he shouted again, and now his shout drowned out all other sounds.

"A leper! There are lepers here!" His shout reverberated, black and threatening, in a moment's breathless silence.

Then rage broke out.

She didn't try to flee.

She was trapped now, behind a wall of people. They dared not come near her. But neither would they let her go until they had given vent to their rage.

"You are unclean. You are death itself. Wench, don't

you understand that? You aren't supposed to sneak around without warning us! We don't want you people in town! Get yourself back to the hospital!"

Tora clung to the basket of fish. Their words struck her, as sharp as knives. Poisonous, dangerous words. She felt terribly dizzy and tired. She couldn't imagine how she would get by them, back to the safety of the house of death.

Then her eyes met Endre's.

At first she couldn't believe what she was seeing. It had to be something she was imagining, because she was alone among hostile strangers. Because she so fervently needed a friend and had no one she could count on.

Then she realized that it really was Endre. But not the Endre she remembered. His tow-colored hair didn't bristle up in the same way. His face was heavier, and he had a yellowish down on his chin and upper lip. His cap, which was cocked boldly over one ear, was new.

Still his glance was the same. That blue glance, which she felt within her mind and which formed his voice bidding her to be calm and brave, bade her remember what they had promised each other: to endure and never back down.

For a moment she felt only relief and happiness, and she wanted to run to him. Then as suddenly there came to her a feeling of shame, and her heart hammered so wildly that she could barely manage to breathe.

Endre didn't know about her! He must not find out now! Endre who had promised his life to her. Just as she had promised her life to him. But she had no life! And she would ruin his if he came near her. She had to get away. Now! Far away. Anywhere at all.

Tora turned sharply with the heavy basket in her arms, stumbled over the edge of the wharf, and fell down into the rocking boat, right into the tub of fresh herring. Fell so hard that herring splattered to all sides and the breath was knocked out of her.

Pain flashed through her neck and back, pain that burned more than the humiliation of floundering helplessly among slimy, smooth herring, while her seeping sores were exposed to the gaping crowd of people and the fisherman thundered in rage above her.

"Get up, you damned monster!"

He roared and shook his fists at her, but he didn't dare touch her.

"Are you also going to poison my catch now! Get out of here. Goddamn you!"

"My good fisherman, be careful about taking God's name in vain. You dare not damn one of God's own chosen children!"

The voice was calm and mild, but it quivered with indignation.

Tora recognized it at once. She looked up, dizzy and nauseous. Saw the well-known black boots, the pastor's billowing black gown, and his warm smile.

The Benefactor stood at the edge of the wharf and

stretched out his soft white hands toward her. "Come, child, let me help you up. Then we'll be going home."

Tora tried to rise, but she reeled and fell. She crawled as fast as she could past the fisherman and up into the bow of the boat. It rocked dangerously while she stretched with all her might to reach his hands.

"So help her now, man!" The pastor's voice was sharp.

"Certainly not," growled the fisherman. "I'll not touch the monster."

"I command you, in God's name!"

It was an order that the fisherman dared not refuse, but it was with obvious loathing and terror that he shoved her up on the edge of the wharf.

The crowd mumbled uneasily and pulled back.

The Benefactor placed himself protectively in front of her and turned toward them.

"How often must I say that you need not fear the lepers! How often must you hear that the illness is not the devil's work? How long must I beg you to show mercy?"

"How do we know that there is nothing to fear?"

Somewhere within the crowd someone had dared to snarl aloud what all of them were thinking.

The pastor took a few steps toward them.

They fell back.

"Because I say so," he said softly. "Oughtn't I to know, I who've dressed so many sores and accompanied so many dead to their graves? Look at me, am I sick?"

He showed them his hands.

It was completely quiet on the wharf. Only the rain splashed evenly and steadily into the waves that thundered against it.

"This poor child is suffering terribly, from both leprosy and the hunger that is ravaging the hospital. She has ventured out among you in order to help her unfortunate brothers and sisters. Have you no pity for her?"

But he knew he would not get an answer.

He turned toward Tora. "Come, I'll walk back with you."

"The fish I bought . . ." she gasped, "the basket of herring . . . the sick . . ."

Her breath came in short gasps. Her lungs burned like fire. She pressed her hands hard against her breast. "Dear . . . help me . . ."

"Here it is, Tora. I'll carry it for you."

Endre stood before her with the basket. She saw that it was brimful of herring.

"No, Endre . . . you must not . . ."

"I want to, Tora. Now that I've found you."

He said it as simply as if they had parted from each other only yesterday. As if death weren't standing between them.

"No . . . !"

It became only a pitiful, long-drawn-out wail, as when the air goes out of a bellows. She could barely hear her own voice.

She gasped for air. Short, wheezing gasps that contracted her dry, sore throat more and more.

She couldn't breathe! There was no more air!

She would die just as gruesomely as Johannes had, with gaping mouth and bulging eyes!

She was going to die . . . here and now! She . . .

"Quick! Carry her! Follow me!"

The pastor had grabbed the basket of fish and used it to make his way through the throng. Right behind him came Endre with Tora in his arms.

The whole way he whisperingly bade her: "Hold on, Tora, hold on . . . Remember your promise, Tora, remember your promise."

She heard his prayer, far away, where the shining mountain plateau and the sky met in a thin band of morning gold.

DEPARTURE

8

eath approached, but she no longer saw a cape-clad old man without a face in the darkness of his hood, but with a scythe resting on a bony shoulder, for death had become painfully present in her every breath.

Tora lay completely still.

She listened to her own rasping breaths.

They were quieter now and deeper. But her lungs still burned like fire when she breathed a little too deeply.

Marthe and the Benefactor had ordered her to lie quietly and rest yet awhile. She had been on a long journey, they said. To death's door.

She knew she had stood on the threshold. She pictured it clearly. It had changed her conception of death.

Death was no longer an old man she could beg for mercy or negotiate with about a postponement. After death had come so close, she had lost all her notions about

that unmerciful reaper who had followed her from childhood. She no longer saw a thin, cape-clad figure, a death's-
head in the dark beneath the hood, an imperious bony
hand stretched out, a scythe that lay ready to harvest life's
crop. Now death was dissolved, formless. Flowed as quietly as a dark river away from her naked anguish.

She now understood she would not be meeting death. It
would overtake her. Not attack or outwit her. Just calmly
and naturally, at its own tempo, stride on past her allotted
time. Death was time. Time that was endlessly old. One
day time would turn toward her and dissolve her within
it. Then her life would be ended. But time would continue. For all eternity.

She knew all that now.

What she did not know was whether death was the end
of everything.

She tried to remember what the pastor at home had said
about resurrection. But the whole time before that spent in
the hospital was as distant as in a dream. She remembered
that it had been difficult to grasp what he meant. Nor had
it concerned her that the figure of wood on the cross above
the altar had risen from the dead. Not then.

All she had cared about then was the growing strength
of the light after the winter's darkness and the new life
sprouting where the sun burned against the church wall.
The only thing she could think about was Endre, who sat
on the men's side of the church with bowed head and
picked at an eagle feather, and her father's empty seat. He

wasn't there then either, even though it was the Easter celebration. He was somewhere down by the fjord where someone needed a fiddler. Didn't he know that she needed him, or didn't he care about her feeling of loss? Would he ever understand that it was no consolation to know that others needed him more? And that one day she would stop hoping and waiting for him to see her and only her.

It was impossible to imagine what could be beyond the end of life. She wished that she could think of herself in Paradise and at resurrection on the Day of Judgment. But she was unable to force her thoughts beyond that point: the end of life.

She now knew quite a lot about the end of life. It meant the end of boundless torture. Liberation from pain that made one rage or beg for mercy. She would probably be able to stand the pain until death overtook her, but never would she wait for a death from strangulation. Never again would she allow herself to experience her breath disappearing and her lungs feeling flat and dead. Never again should her throat feel as if it were closed with a cork. Never again would she hear the echo of Johannes's jaws snapping like broken twigs when she forced his mouth closed before laying him in the coffin.

Never would they have to do the same with her.

She would choose her own death before that.

The Benefactor had sat with her the whole night after that terrible incident at the fish market. He massaged her throat, which was knotted with cramps, while Marthe took care that the porridge poultices on Tora's wheezing chest were always red hot.

"Your body will begin to work for you again, God willing," he comforted her.

Tora noticed nothing. She fought only to escape choking. She wanted to flee. To death or to life. No matter where. If only her suffering stopped.

She knew that Endre had been there the whole time and had warmed her ice-cold hands. When, for a short moment, she had gained consciousness, she had seen her stubby, oozing hands in his healthy, smooth hands. She had tried to shove him away and to say that he should leave before it was too late, but she never managed to gather enough strength to do so.

All night she would drift from the cool, dark horizon where she herself was weightless to that fever-hot, pain-ridden body in the bed. Her visits to the little room had been short and clear, like glimpses of sharp light in pitch blackness.

She caught half-words and broken sentences, whispering, uneasy voices. The Benefactor, Endre, and Marthe sat by the bed and talked about her. Endre talked a lot. She heard her mother's, her father's, and her own name mentioned.

She wanted to tell them to send Endre away from her and the death within her. Death should not be allowed to accompany Endre. He was strong and young. He should live for a long time after her death.

When she awakened, the little room was completely dark and she was alone.

The bed was warm and damp. The sharp odor of tar and green potash soap burned her nose, and she felt something sticky weighing on her breast. For a moment she was gripped by panic. Had they prepared her for burial already? Washed her in tar and green potash soap, wrapped her in a shroud that she had perhaps sewn herself!

Carefully she moved her hands. There were no flowers between her fingers. She laid her hands on her breast and realized that the sticky mass was a porridge poultice. A soothing green compress, such as she herself had helped Marthe put on so many of the ill who were stricken with consumption.

Her relief made her careless. She drew in a deep breath in order to sit up. She had totally forgotten what the punishment was for sudden movements.

It was as if someone had driven a spike into her. Streams of pain spread throughout her body. Blindingly white pain that, with a thundering strike, sent a chill to her heart.

Slowly, slowly, she came back to herself.

She knew immediately that the pain had lain in wait for her.

She gasped with terror.

There was someone with her.

Someone who had coaxed her back with soft caresses.
She could feel them now, hands that stroked and petted.
She dared not move or open her eyes to see. The pain
watched for the least movement. Prepared to slash at her
again. Perhaps harder, wilder.

It was good just to float like this, quietly. Feel tiredness
spread heavily through her body, while Marthe stroked
and stroked her. Big, kind Marthe, who did not have billowing red hair and wildness in her heart but who
watched over her as if Tora were her own child.

Slowly, slowly, she drifted toward the edge of consciousness again.

Then she felt the change. The hands stroked no longer.

They had stopped at her chest. The porridge poultice
was ripped off and her breasts bared. A hard fist squeezed
one of her naked breasts. The nipple shrank in pain. The
other fist ripped off the blanket and grabbed her hard in
the crotch.

Tora opened her eyes and screamed as the pains flashed
from her lungs to her brain.

Screamed into the man's face with its beard streaked
brown with tobacco juice and its stench of beer and lust.
Screamed toward the body with its naked member.

Screamed and screamed until the dark light blinded
her terror.

et out, you monster! Get out before I fetch the pastor! Have you no shame, you damned peasant!"

It was Marthe shouting. Marthe who furiously pulled the heavy body of the man away and placed herself protectively in front of Tora.

He mumbled something or other. She could not hear what he said. But Marthe's biting answer she heard clearly:

"Don't lie, peasant! Never in all the world did this little girl ask you to come here. But I can guess who did send you, and she shall have to answer for it, the witch! You, I'll report to the authorities, do you hear? The whole town shall learn that you who damn the leprous so loudly sneak in here and . . . and . . . entertain yourself with the poor things. Even with a child who is out of her senses with pain. May God grant that you'll be punished hard for this!"

She would surely have continued to revile him for quite

a long time if she had not been so worried that the other sick people would become agitated.

He got to his feet and slunk quickly toward the door.

Tora opened her eyes. As he disappeared through the doorway, she saw his face and recognized him. She sobbed.

Marthe bent over her. "I'll come back at once, child. Lie completely still until I have gotten the swine out and have properly locked the gate.

She brought with her a steaming porridge poultice and a bowl of fish soup.

"There, now we'll take care of you properly. Don't move, otherwise the pain will start again!"

"He . . . it was he . . ."

"Now now. I know, poor child. Luckily nothing happened."

Marthe talked calmly and gently as she took care of her.

Tora felt the pains retreat to a steady aching. Her heart began to beat again in a regular rhythm.

Nothing had happened. Nothing more than that she would always fear shadows that filled the doorway with a dense darkness, and she would never sleep again without feeling the weight of the body of a panting man above her.

"You must eat, Tora, you haven't eaten any food for days."

Marthe lifted Tora's head with one hand and brought the bowl to her mouth with the other.

The soup was warm and smelled good, but nausea rose

from her stomach and filled her mouth. Fear made it impossible for her to swallow.

Tora looked pleadingly at Marthe.

"Then we'll wait a little," answered Marthe softly. "In the meantime, we can talk a bit about other things. Maybe you don't know what is wrong with you? No, you don't have consumption. Thank the Lord, otherwise we would have probably lost you during the hemorrhaging. But you have lung disease, or pneumonia, as the Benefactor says it's called in medicine. The terrible fever attacks and kills many of the lepers. You've seen that yourself, of course. But we sometimes manage to check it. With God's help."

Marthe grew silent.

Tora cautiously touched her hand.

"I was so afraid of losing you. You've become so dear to me, Tora. I've prayed to God to be merciful, for I can't yet bear to let you go. He has heard my prayers."

"Thank you," whispered Tora.

"I'll never leave you." Marthe turned away.

It was like an echo of Tora's mother's voice.

To think that such love was again to be found. A love that made her feel worthwhile. Not beautiful, for she wasn't. Nor would she ever be so again. Just more and more disgusting. But no matter how helpless and repulsive she became, love would be there for her.

"Don't imagine that I am the only one here who is fond of you, my sweet, beautiful child. For you are beautiful beneath the leprosy. Your soul is beautiful. It will become only more beautiful and strong as the time draws near. The time that the Lord has determined for you to be brought to heaven."

Like a refreshing wind, the words rushed through her, and at once she knew that her splintered life would be whole again. Her body, that pain-filled sheath that she scorned so intensely and tried in every way to flee, was the soul's dwelling. If only her soul were beautiful, it could fill her body and she would feel herself to be whole.

Were God and death one and the same? Was it actually as Marthe said, that God would fetch her to Him? That He was Time, which marched to its own beat, which would overtake her? Then all was not ended at the end of life. Then the beginning lay beyond death.

Resurrection, she thought suddenly.

She knew nothing about it. She must find out.

"Can you read, Marthe?"

Marthe looked at her with surprise. "No, I have the Lord's words within me. I don't need to read. Not many here at the hospital have learned how, and still they are members of Jesus Christ's elect." She rose suddenly. "That, you can't say about one of those here who can read! She must be in league with the devil himself!"

Marthe angrily snapped her mouth shut and grabbed the soup bowl. "You can eat a little now." It was an order.

Tora nodded. She swallowed noisily.

"It tastes wonderful."

"It's good, isn't it? It's your herring, remember that. Herring that kept hunger at bay for several days. Herring that you worked so hard to get in trade from . . ." Marthe again became silent.

Tora nearly smiled. Did Marthe actually believe that she didn't know who had tried to force his way with her? Or that she didn't understand who had sent the monster? She knew and would never forget. It felt good to have loving and motherly Marthe protecting her, trying to conceal what Marthe didn't think would be good for Tora to know. It was as if Tora were lying on a soft lap and being rocked like a child. There was even enough room for her fear and loneliness.

"Endre is a fine boy. He is very much in love with you, Tora."

"Marthe! Help me. He mustn't . . ."

Tora tried to sit up, but the pain kept her back.

Marthe determinedly pushed her back in the bed.

"No, it was clear to all the world that you didn't want Endre to be infected. Both the Benefactor and I tried to do as you wished; we bade him, as earnestly as we could, to go, but he refused. He had to be certain that you would live, he said. Not until then would he go. You know, Tora, he wouldn't budge from your side for several days. Only when I needed help with the heavy washtubs."

Marthe grew silent for a time.

"There have been terribly many sick and dying during this time," she continued. "I thought it would perhaps frighten Endre away, but no. He sat with you just as faithfully as ever. He warmed you and dried the perspiration off you and helped me to wash you."

Marthe smiled broadly when she saw Tora turning blood-red.

"I know that you are not man and wife, but it isn't difficult to see that you are mates. For life, aren't you?"

Tora nodded slowly.

"Not until the worst was past and we were certain that we could keep you did he go. But," she continued gently, "he'll come back one day, Tora. That I'm quite certain of. And you shall wait for him and make him welcome, for you mustn't deny him the right to love you as he wants to."

It was quiet for quite a long time while Marthe waited for Tora's answer.

"I know," she said at last.

Marthe nodded, satisfied, and continued: "The day that your good Endre met you at the fish market he had just gotten a berth aboard a Dutch ship. Luckily, it remained at anchor here in the harbor for several days waiting for a cargo of dried fish while he was here at the hospital. He has sailed now, but he left a grand gift for the hospital. A whole bushel of rye, a bushel of wheat, and many pounds of dried fish."

Marthe stuck a hand in the pocket of her apron and showed Tora a fistful of shining silver dollars. "He left you all his wages. The captain of the Dutch ship was persuaded to pay them in advance. It's nearly unfathomable that such goodhearted people are to be found! You are lucky to be so loved, child. But, then, of course, you deserve it, I know."

Tora couldn't look at her.

Endre had left. That was how she wanted it. But he had left behind him an emptiness that nothing could fill.

Perhaps she had managed to spare him from the cruelty of leprosy. She deeply hoped so. Then it was worth the sacrifice.

"He asked me to say that you must never forget the pact. Then he gave you this."

Marthe stretched out her hand.

Tora grasped the object and recognized it with her fingers.

It was exactly as she remembered. Smooth, slender, and sun-bleached. The joint of the eagle's wing was beautiful life beneath dead flesh.

Tora turned toward the wall and cried silently.

ora knocked hard on the door of the little bedroom. She waited a long time.

Mistress Dybendal was in there, that she knew. She could be nowhere else, for now she was not even able to get over to the beautiful chair with the high back on her own. She was helpless, and Tora was the only one who would voluntarily tend and feed her.

"Can you actually stand to do that?" Marthe had asked worriedly when Tora had offered. "You who've just been so ill yourself? Surely it would be better for you to take care of Britta and Christine, good and devout women? They aren't like that . . . that . . ."

"I can manage it and want to do it," interrupted Tora firmly. "And I can manage it alone."

Tora could well understand that it put Marthe in a bad mood just to think of the Mistress. For as the Mistress had become more ill, she had become more furious, and she took her anger out on Marthe. There was no end to the poisonous curses that she let rain down on Marthe if she just appeared in the doorway.

Tora knew that such behavior bothered Marthe terribly, for she was convinced that the Mistress was possessed by Satan, and she feared for her own soul in the presence of the power of the Evil One.

Tora herself was frightened of the Mistress, but not for the same reason that Marthe was. She was more curious than frightened, really, for that raging young woman was a mystery to her. She couldn't understand how such a sick, emaciated person had the strength to keep her rage so red hot. And Tora well knew how much strength it took. The Mistress was dying, but she refused to surrender herself to God. She was suffering terribly, but she rejected all sympathy. She had to know that everyone desired her death just as intensely as she herself desired to die.

It was impossible to fathom that she wanted to live like that. Even more difficult to grasp was how she could stand to be so alone behind that wall of hatred. That wall she herself had built. And still Tora realized that she envied the Mistress her iron-hard will to be herself, wholly and fully. Despite what others thought. That was something she herself did not have the courage to do. But then she did not come from a wealthy and distinguished family either. Who would ever bother about what a poor farm girl felt, a girl who couldn't even write her own name?

It distressed Tora that she envied and admired the Mistress and simultaneously loathed her. She felt trapped by her longing to understand a mystery that she knew the Mistress would never voluntarily unveil to her. It irritated her that she could not stop speculating about what the Mistress was hiding. After a while, she became completely certain that the Mistress had a reason for pushing everyone away. There was something in her glance, a flash of triumph and relief, which Tora had seen when the sobbing Marthe was chased out the door. Could it be that the Mistress knew a secret, a truth about death that was so wonderful that nothing else mattered? Not even horrible suffering and others' hatred?

That was the mystery which daily drove Tora up the steep stairs to Mistress Dybendal with food and drink, buckets of green soapy water and tar, clean bandages and glass cups with the leeches that she had taught herself to place on the Mistress's legs where the surgeon had sawn them off. Shining leeches that attached themselves tightly to the vessels around the stumps of her legs and grew dark with blood as they pulsated in their own nearly invisible rhythm of sucking.

Nothing made Tora feel so unwell as the sight of the leeches. When she placed the cups with the leeches on the Mistress's skin, her own skin got goosebumps from her disgust at their tiny movements, which she knew all too well.

Only the thought of the mystery enabled her to bear the drudgery, stench, and stream of poisonous curses. The mystery and the reward that she had so carefully planned how to obtain. The reward, worth all her patient waiting to see the first little crack in the Mistress's wall of defense, would be the moment when the Mistress admitted that she was dependent on her care. Tora thought that the moment would arrive when she knocked on the door and the Mistress asked her to come in.

Tora again knocked hard and waited a long time.

Then she knocked for the third time.

She had prepared for this contest ever since that first day she had come to tend the Mistress alone. It was a battle of wills, which no one knew about. Nor did anyone know that all her self-sacrificing care of the Mistress was done for the sake of a reward. It was fine that they believed she was kind to a fault. It didn't bother her at all as long as she got what she wanted.

She knocked again. For the fourth time without an answer.

She waited patiently. She might knock as many as ten times without getting an answer. Not until then did she go in and start to tend the Mistress.

The first days the Mistress had lain immobile, staring at the ceiling. She refused to look at Tora, no matter what she did. Twice Tora had purposely dropped things on the floor, but the Mistress wasn't to be tricked. She stared just as fixedly. Up at the ceiling, past her or through her. For the most part she was completely silent. When she spoke, only a flood of insults and abuse came out. Never a complaint, no matter how great her pain was. The wall around her feelings was impenetrable.

Never had Tora met anyone like this strange woman, so mysterious and so infinitely distant. Never had any person caused such a confusion of feelings in her.

How she disliked the arrogance and wickedness! She had not the least bit of bad conscience for wanting to exploit the Mistress. It was just what she deserved. But at the same time Tora's admiration grew. And her sympathy became only stronger. The Mistress was afraid. As deathly afraid as Tora had ever seen anyone be. Why did she think it so frightening that Tora never got even, would not be chased away, not give up her attempts to reach her?

Tora found no answer. But she continued to do everything she could to catch the Mistress's eye. At the same time, she felt more and more ashamed, as if she were spying on her. The thought of the Mistress as helpless and frightened, fighting not to be exposed, haunted her continually. Tora always pictured her clearly. How expectant and fearful she was.

Days passed without anything happening, other than Tora's having to strive harder each day to care for her and feed her in the usual way, without feeling bothered by the eruptions of anger, which were becoming more and more desperate. Without succumbing to the desire to stroke her hair and say that she didn't mean to hurt her. Tora had to force herself to leave just as silently as she had come. But she might remain standing outside the door for a long time while her tears ran, and she wondered whether she was crying for herself or for the woman in there.

Tora was certain that neither of them would be able to explain why she continued to fight for control with nothing but the strength of her will as a weapon, why neither of them could be the first to give up. She knew, too, that each of them admired and hated the other's persistence, and they both knew that they shared something that was perhaps dangerous and harmful.

One more week passed tensely. Tora was aware of how exhausted she was from the toil and the battle. She was at the point of giving up. Should she stop caring for the Mistress? Let her swim or sink? Someone else could care for her, for example, Ranneveig, the harsh night nurse. It probably wouldn't matter; the Mistress would surely die soon anyway.

Even the thought hurt.

Perhaps the wisest thing would be to tell the Mistress everything, about the reward she wanted for nursing her and the rest of it. No, she couldn't. The first was too humiliating to tell. The second she had no words for.

She saw no other recourse than to continue, wait, and hope.

Then one morning when she came in after having knocked over and over again and having waited a long time in between, the Mistress lay looking at her.

"Why don't you just come right in?" Her voice was dark with anger and sorrow.

Tora quickly turned and pretended she had dropped something on the floor. The Mistress must not see how relieved she was! Must not guess how near the Mistress herself had been to winning their power struggle.

When Tora turned around, she knew that her face did not reveal what she was feeling. She looked the Mistress straight in the eyes. For a long time. And suddenly she saw that the Mistress had understood everything anyway. She had understood that it was not just a battle of wills but a carefully planned contest for which Tora had determined the rules.

The Mistress's eyes were suddenly filled with tears. But she did not turn away. She continued staring, as if she wanted to say, *So you have won your first victory. But do you know how it feels to be deceived?*

Tora shrank back. She heard that silent accusation like an echo behind all her thoughts. She tried to convince herself that it was not her fault that the Mistress felt deceived. But it became increasingly difficult to justify continuing her game when she knew how painful it was for the Mistress.

After that, the Mistress stopped scolding her completely. She just lay still, following Tora's least movement with a watchful look.

Tora could no longer bear to meet her glance.

Tora lifted her hand to knock, but suddenly she could not.

It had to end. After all, she had already won. Why couldn't she just go in and ask the Mistress for the favor?

Then she heard the call. Weak, reluctant.

The Mistress had given up the battle!

Tora experienced a giddy feeling of triumph. She had forced the Mistress to do what she least wanted to. Not even the pastor had managed to do what she, a lowly farm girl, had done. But she had to proceed carefully now, not show that she knew that she had the upper hand. Otherwise, the Mistress might withdraw completely. She was just as wary as the hawk that Tora and Endre had once tried to tame.

The first time the hawk had voluntarily taken food from their hands they had been cautious, taking care not to be too hasty. The bird had to believe that it was coming to them of its own free will, Endre had said. They had failed with the hawk, but it was not just their fault. She still felt bad when she thought about it. She and Endre wanted to tame the hawk only in order to use it, and they had enticed it with trust. They had not cared what the hawk felt when it was deceived.

lowly Tora opened the door and walked in. Triumph had a bitter aftertaste.

The eyes of the woman in the bed were wary and expectant.

"Thanks for asking me in," said Tora. She quickly smiled and looked away.

She began the morning routine, precisely as usual. But nothing was as usual any longer. Everything had changed. She wanted to say so, but she did not know how to begin. Not as long as the Mistress's eyes followed her and said accusingly: *I am in your power. What do you want of me?*

Tora concentrated on lifting the Mistress's head to make it easier to get the soup into the gaping cavity of her mouth. For the first time she thought how terribly the Mistress was suffering and how humiliating this had to be for her.

Tora's hand, which otherwise usually held the spoon so still, shook as if she herself had a fever. And she couldn't stand to watch as the Mistress strove to swallow without spilling. How she fought to keep her dignity.

The whole time, while washing her, changing the linens and bandages, and at last lifting her over to the beautiful chair so the bed could be changed, she felt the Mistress's eyes burning against her face. Heard the question that the woman couldn't make herself ask: *Why can't you say what you want of me?*

Tora was deeply relieved that the Mistress had not dared to ask, for she was not capable of answering. Not capable of exposing her shame. Everything had changed now. So different from when she had planned to make the Mistress so dependent on her help that it would be easy to say *Teach me to read* without fearing that the Mistress would say no.

It had been terribly wrong to force her to admit her dependence. She simply had not understood how much pride meant to the Mistress. But Tora, who was so proud herself, ought, of course, to have understood! For the first time in her life, she felt herself to be cruel. It was like being covered with mud and not being able to wash herself. She regretted it, but there was no way to make up for it. No way back.

After that the Mistress called, "Come in," as soon as Tora knocked.

Like an obedient child, thought Tora, and felt herself chastened.

She had to force herself to go in to those watchful, knowing eyes.

Several days passed before she managed to meet the Mistress's glance, and then she became first frightened and next uncertain. Was it a smile she saw in those eyes? It wasn't easy to tell, since she couldn't see if that horrible mouth was smiling. But surely she would be able to hear it in the woman's voice. If only she would talk! If only she would mock and rage as before! But she was silent and expectant, while Tora struggled with her bad conscience.

One day when Tora opened the door carefully and hesitated an extra long time about coming in, the Mistress said loudly and firmly: "Come here and sit on my chair. We must talk."

It came as such a surprise that Tora obeyed without thinking. But she sat on the edge of the chair, without daring to move.

"Take it easy. The chair won't bite. I won't either. You deserve some rest after all the work you've been doing for me."

Tora shivered. But the voice was without a trace of malice.

"You'll get the chair when I am dead," she continued. "Then I'll be free of debt."

Tora could feel that she turned flaming red, and she

saw herself as a carrion bird waiting for its prey to die. She had to bite her lip not to start crying in torrents. She was not the person the Mistress believed her to be! She hadn't meant it that way! But it seemed like greed, she now realized.

"Did you really believe that I wouldn't see through you? That I didn't immediately understand that you expected a reward for all your self-sacrificing effort?"

She spoke slowly. She had to strain to pronounce the words clearly.

Without looking at Tora, she continued: "Oh yes, you see, I recognized a parasite in the offing the first time you came by. My whole life I have been surrounded by self-sacrificing menials. Like you, they all expected a reward. You think I am loathsome toward your friend Marthe, don't you?"

Tora nodded slightly.

"If only you knew how many foolish women have tried to ensnare me with motherly concern. Marthe is like the hypocritical nuns in the cloister in Florence. I was ill and unhappy and alone. They tended me and said they loved me. But actually they only wanted to make me so dependent on their care that I would be an easy prey to their wishes. But they miscalculated. I saw through them before they managed to make me a Bride of Christ."

She suddenly laughed. "What do you have to say for yourself, my fine Samaritan friend?"

Nothing. There was nothing she could say. Her shame

had become still greater. How could she have imagined that the Mistress would let herself be taken in? Suddenly all her plans seemed very foolish, very childish. And everything had been turned upside down.

Tora rose.

She had to get away. Immediately. Never would she see this person again.

"No, don't flee, please," said the Mistress seriously. "That will solve nothing. After all, Tora, you now know that I need you. You are the only one who has gotten me to admit it. I know that you need me, and that makes us equals. Can't you, then, trust me enough to tell me what it is you want as a reward?"

The word was like the lash of a whip, even though a reward was all that she herself had thought about. The entire time. It was no use dodging it anymore. She had to tell the truth. It was, in spite of everything, better than what the Mistress was imagining.

"I want to learn to read," she eventually mumbled.

"What? Speak up, wench. I can't hear what you're saying!"

She had dreamed so long about the moment when the Mistress would gratefully offer to teach her to read. Now it was she who had to beg. All at once her throat felt too tight for words. She strove for a long time to force them out: "Teach me to read. I beg you."

"Is that all?!"

Tora nodded and looked away.

"In other words, that's nearly everything," said the Mistress dryly.

"No! Don't misunderstand, Mistress Dybendal! I don't want anything else. Nothing that you own. I promise! I just want to be allowed to learn from you. Please."

Tora couldn't manage to say more.

The Mistress was silent while Tora cried. Tora didn't look at her a single time.

"The worst is past now. Don't cry anymore," she said quietly. "You'll have your reward, if only I have enough time left. But I want you to do something for me."

"What is it?"

Tora stopped sniffing.

"Don't call me Mistress Dybendal. Nothing about that name is right. I want you to call me Sunniva. That's my first name."

"I promise!"

"You must leave now, Tora. I am tired."

Tora hurried out, relieved to get away.

In the darkness outside the door, she remained sitting with her face in her hands for a long time.

They had spent many days getting the young hawk to come voluntarily and to eat fearlessly from their hands. They had not attempted to care for its injured wing, for they knew that it would make the bird uneasy. Besides, it managed to care for the wing quite well itself, and it was easy to see that the bird would soon be able to fly again.

They had agreed on taking it home with them before it could fly and keeping it hidden in the barn. Endre had made a cage for it, but they didn't try to force it in, just waited patiently until it wanted to go in on its own. It took a long time before it dared to hop into the cage to get its food. After that, it hopped in and out as if it were the most natural thing in the world. It would sit quietly in the cage for a long time, staring at them with a straightforward, trusting look, completely ignorant of what was going to happen.

They had only thought of having it in the cage. Had only wanted to tame it so that it could catch mice. If only Mons hadn't come, if only he had not tried to catch the hawk, if only Endre and Tora had not begun to fight with him—perhaps the hawk would not have tried to escape from them.

Tora could still see it clearly: the bird, which shot toward the ceiling of the hay barn, desperate to find a way out, one wing powerlessly beating in the attempt to keep itself aloft. The bird, which fell, fell toward the knife-sharp hayfork; the pierced breast of the bird, which burned red in the sunlight, while its wings slowly stopped quivering.

She could still feel her sorrow and shame.

ou have not told me why you want to learn to read." Sunniva looked searchingly at her and waited.

Tora pretended not to have heard the question, just bent even closer to the yellowed pages of the thick Bible. The letters were beautiful but, for the most part, were still secretive and foreign.

"Why won't you answer?"

"Everyone wants to learn to read," answered Tora at last. Evasively. She felt her cheeks growing warm.

"That, I don't believe. At any rate, it isn't like that here at the hospital. Why should any of them bother about learning to read when they are going to die soon? Answer me that, Tora!"

"I've already told you, don't you remember? I want to learn!" It sounded more angry than she had meant it to.

"I don't believe it's so simple. I know you want to learn for a very particular reason."

Tora heard that Sunniva was enjoying herself, and she regretted not having found a good answer at once. Now Sunniva wouldn't stop. She would go on teasing and heckling Tora until she told the truth.

"Then do you want me to guess?"

"No! But promise me you won't laugh. Then I'll explain."

"I promise."

She first had to tell about the church and the parish pastor at home and all the wonderful things that he said were to be read in the Holy Book, and about Granny, who had said that God could never forgive Tora's mother her mortal sin.

"I want to know what God really thinks. Does that sound strange?"

Sunniva was silent for a fairly long time. Then she said quietly, "You want to know whether God loves you, isn't that so?"

When Tora did not answer, she continued harshly: "You can't understand why He is letting you die. And why death must be so terrible. You can't imagine what sins you've committed. You can't bring yourself to believe that it is a good and loving God who is doing this to you. Isn't that true?"

"You're saying that I don't believe in God!"

"No," answered Sunniva slowly. "You're saying so. I'm

only asking whether you doubt that God loves you when He punishes you so harshly."

"I have to go now." Tora rose abruptly. "Marthe needs me."

"Tora! Why are you so afraid to ask and to doubt? You've a right to do so. It's your life, and you'll meet death all alone. Naturally you want to know whether you can trust in God's being with you."

"It's easy enough for you to talk! Everyone knows that you are godless. No one dares touch you because you belong to a wealthy and powerful family! But no one is protecting me."

"Oh, is that so."

Sunniva began to laugh. That old scornful laughter which made Tora feel smaller than a louse.

"Indeed, then it is better that you take yourself down to Marthe. You aren't mature enough to talk about such important things as your own life and your own death. Come back when you have stopped whining!"

She turned toward the wall. Even her back expressed her scorn.

Tora stood for a moment indecisively.

What she had said was mean. And terribly stupid, for there was no one else really to depend on than her. If only Sunniva knew what it was like to doubt and wonder about everything: whether there was a God, whether there was a life after death, why she had been born at all, what was the reason for dying so terribly.

Why didn't she dare admit to Sunniva that she doubted? She didn't know. Maybe Sunniva was right. Maybe she wasn't grown up enough to talk. She left.

In her dream that night she knelt before Granny and felt the lashes of the whip whine across her back. Granny struck and struck and struck. Still, Tora refused to admit her sin.

"May I come in?"

It was the first time Tora had asked. The question surprised her nearly as much as it did Sunniva.

"Of course."

Her voice was mild. Her eyes nearly sparkled with laughter. She was sitting halfway up in bed, with the heavy Bible in her lap.

How in the world had she gotten to it? She must have struggled half the night, for Tora remembered that she had laid the Bible down on the chair before she ran out and the chair was more than an arm's length away from the bed. Getting it must have cost her a good deal of strength and great pain.

"I have something for you," said Sunniva.

"I, too," said Tora, and handed her the bowl full of bright yellow coltsfoot that she had picked in the meadow. "Can you forgive me?"

Sunniva nodded. "Come closer," she said. "Let me feel the rain in your hair."

Tora knelt by the headboard and placed her head in the

hollow of Sunniva's throat. She felt the short stumps of Sunniva's fingers running through her hair. "I trust you. I can talk about this only with you," she whispered.

"Don't you think I feel the same?" said Sunniva softly. "We have so little time together, and there is so much I want to teach you to think about in the time you have left. Thoughts and dreams are a wonderful way to travel, Tora. It costs nothing, neither money nor pain. You can be as imprisoned and chained as we are and still experience the most fantastic worlds. Do you understand, Tora, that's why I want to teach you to read."

Tora nodded. Sunniva's hair tickled her nose. Hair that reminded her of her mother's.

"That's why I want to talk to you about God. I know that you are in doubt and feel guilty and afraid. I can't lessen your doubt, but I can help you to think a bit more clearly. Do you understand?"

She nodded again. It felt safe and good to be lying there like that.

"May I read something to you now?" asked Sunniva. "I am not certain you will like hearing it, but it may help you. This is what the Holy Book says about you and me, Tora. This is the Lord's decree to Moses and Aaron about the unclean illness of leprosy."

She opened the Bible and slowly started to read:

When a man shall have in the skin of his flesh a rising, a
scab, or bright spot, and it be in the skin of his flesh like

the plague of leprosy; then he shall be brought unto
Aaron the priest, or unto one of his sons the priests.
And the priest shall look on the plague in the skin of the
flesh: and when the hair in the plague is turned white,
and the plague in sight be deeper than the skin of his
flesh, it is a plague of leprosy: and the priest shall look on
him, and pronounce him unclean.

"But . . ." Tora sat up.

"What is it?"

"Nothing," mumbled Tora.

"Shall I continue?"

"I don't want to hear any more."

"There is a great deal about what God ordained that the priests should do with people like us. Therefore, we are where we are today, and all people fear us and loathe even the thought that we exist. Therefore, they shut us in and declare us dead to the whole world. Do you know that I am listed as dead in the church register? Perhaps you, too, are *dead* in your church register at home."

"I said I didn't want to hear any more!" Tora howled. She went to the window and stared out. It took a long time before her tears dried.

"Tora! I want to know what you are thinking."

"Nothing."

Her voice sounded harder than she intended.

It was quiet for a long time.

"I don't understand," said Tora after a while. "For example, the part about the white hair."

"Nor do I, my friend. I do not have white hair on my boils, nor have I seen anyone who does, and I have met many lepers. Do you know anyone with boils that are depressions in the skin? Have you seen anything other than disgusting reddish-violet lumps?" said Sunniva derisively.

"It does not mean anything one way or the other," said Tora hesitantly. "We are lepers no matter what."

"That's one thing," said Sunniva sharply. "And it's the reason that I wanted to read that to you. Our illness is described incorrectly in the Holy Book. Either God made a mistake when He gave his command about leprosy or Moses did when he interpreted God's word."

"You are mad!"

"Mad for daring to tell you that I doubt that everything in the Bible is true and right? I feel that I am quite sensible in asking whether God can make mistakes about small things! If He can, He can make mistakes about larger things, too, isn't that true?"

"I don't know if I dare," said Tora honestly.

"Say it aloud, you mean," said Sunniva dryly. "For you're certainly thinking it. Just as I do, you doubt whether God exists. Just as I am, you are afraid that you must believe, because death is waiting. Who indeed dares to believe that hell does not exist? For that is the worst thing, isn't it? The thought that hell actually exists and you will be doomed to eternal torture. Worse even than doubting that God is always good and is always right."

Tora nodded, trembling. "The most terrible thought of all. Then there is no way out. No end to the hell here on earth, just something much worse in store. It is much easier just to say to myself that God's ways are inscrutable and that His will is hidden from human beings."

"There's one thing you can believe anyway, without needing to fear God's punishment," said Sunniva, and laughed. "Pastors, my friend, are people, and they make mistakes. Also about God's word. Sometimes because they don't know enough, other times because it serves their purposes, their purses, or their stomachs. That's something history tells a lot about. I learned a great deal about it in the cloister in Italy. One day I'll tell you about Copernicus and Galileo and the other great thinkers who knew things that the priests didn't like."

"Will you?" said Tora hopefully. She loved stories.

"For certain. But not now. It's time for school."

13

ora sat by the window, bent over the Bible. She spelled her way through the first words of the account of creation. She didn't know how many times she had struggled now to get through the difficult words.

Sunniva had said that it was best for her to learn to read from the Bible. Both because it was full of wonderful tales and because the print was large and clear. She was undoubtedly right, but Tora thought it was extremely tiring anyway. The muscles of her neck hurt, and the letters danced before her eyes. Each time she tried to read the words aloud, she found that the letters refused to stay in place.

She stopped in the midst of *the beginning* and sighed wearily.

"Perhaps you thought it was easy? Well, now you've

learned your first lesson. It is difficult to learn to read and write."

The voice from the bed sounded almost cheerful.

Tora clenched her teeth and concentrated on spelling *the beginning* once again. It irritated her that Sunniva was so vigilantly attentive. It irritated her still more that Sunniva was always right and couldn't refrain from openly reveling in it.

At any rate, there was one thing Tora had learned by now: she had to beware of expressing her impatience out loud.

It was laborious learning the art of reading, but it was also far more exciting than she had dreamed. She discovered that the very first time she opened the Bible, after she had carefully scraped all the tallow off its magnificent cover.

The black letters, in their carefully ordered rows on the pages, were beautiful. She felt a stab of happy expectation, for every page was as enticing as a mysterious landscape. She became terribly impatient to learn the secrets hidden behind the letters.

But Sunniva restrained her. "You have to be patient, Tora. You must learn to crawl before you can walk. You have to be at home with the alphabet before you can read. You must be able to see the A before you when you hear it spoken and hear the sound of the B when you see it on the paper. You have to be able to recognize each letter, no matter whether it is printed or written by hand. Next you'll learn the difference between the language you speak and the language that is written. Not until you know all that are you ready to learn to walk."

Sunniva laughed out loud. "Was that asking a little too much? You should see your face. I've never seen such disappointment."

"I am not disappointed!" she lied. "It's just a little . . . demanding."

"And who has said that it should be easy to learn the noblest art of all? It is difficult. What is best is generally what is most difficult to attain. But when you master the art, you are free. Free to think for yourself and to learn about others' thoughts, free to dream and travel, anywhere at all in the past, present, or future. Isn't that a wonderful reward, one worth the effort it takes?"

Tora became warm. It was good to see how happy it made Sunniva to help her. It was as if the teaching had given Sunniva energy and life.

"Just hurry slowly, Tora! Use your time and mine well, and I promise you a joyful time before your own end."

Tora tried to use their time in the best way possible.

Every day she got up early and prepared food for Sunniva before Marthe took over the kitchen. Occasionally she could sneak out an extra bowl of gruel or a bit of dry bread that she knew Marthe wouldn't notice. Marthe was particular that all the sick should share precisely alike in the little there was to be divided. Certainly Sunniva wasn't to get a crumb more.

When the weather was tolerably good, Tora went out to pick wildflowers in the meadow. She knew that Sunniva enjoyed the presence of the dewy flowers. When Tora came up, Sunniva always lay waiting, always with a plan prepared for Tora's school day, which they discussed as Tora got her ready.

Tora was happy about that; then she could avoid thinking about how thin Sunniva had become and what difficulty she now had in breathing. When the chores were done, Tora sat down on the chair by the window and started her work. Until the twilight disappeared, she read and wrote, went at it hammer and tongs. Almost without noticing it, she made great progress.

Suddenly one day she discovered that the alphabet had become a rhythmic jingle that ran on by itself as soon as she had thought A. It was as if the alphabet had always been a part of her memory. Another miracle had occurred within the pages of the books, without her knowing exactly when it had happened. The letters had simply transformed themselves from black signs, which danced meaninglessly on the pages, into words with a meaning she recognized. *"Wrath, sun, wind, and tears,"* she read aloud, and shouted with joy over her own good fortune. Because she knew exactly how the words felt. Most amazing was the thought that the words in the

Bible, which were so alive and familiar to her, had been written so long, long ago. Those who had once formed the words had died several hundred years before she was born. But now their words were alive and fresh again because she was reading them. That gave her a wonderful feeling of being a part of something that was very great and old.

She had to tell Sunniva.

"You've discovered Time, Tora. Isn't that wonderful? The books allow you to hear the voices and thoughts of people who have lived long before you, in entirely different times and worlds than the one you know."

It became even more important to practice reading after that.

Only the writing bothered her. Not because it was difficult to write, but because it was painful. Her swollen fingers refused to obey when she took hold of the slate pencil, and even when she forced them, her writing was but a grotesque caricature of the elegant lettering in the book that Sunniva had given her.

It made her angry that she was not able to master it. She didn't want to write in such an ugly way in that beautiful book. It was tall and slender, bound in fine calfskin. Many of the pages were filled with Sunniva's delicate, ornate handwriting, and many pages were blank. Sunniva had said that Tora could write her own story on them.

"When you read what I have written, you'll get to know

a great deal about me that no one else knows. That ought to tempt you to work harder, you who are so curious."

She laughed a little when she said it, and a bit of time passed before Tora understood that Sunniva had given her precious secret to her.

"Thank you!"

"But remember, you don't get to read it until I'm dead, for I want none of your questions. And you must promise never to show it to anyone else. But do continue to write in the book. That would please me greatly."

Sunniva breathed deeply. It sounded nearly like a sob.

"You can trust me," whispered Tora. She wasn't able to say aloud that she would destroy the book before she herself died.

Something had changed.

Tora knew the minute she came in.

Sunniva lay as usual with her face turned toward the door. Her red hair gleamed in the sharp sun of morning. Her eyes were shut, but she was not sleeping.

"Tora? You must light the candle so you can see—to work. It's getting dark early," she said.

Tora reached her in one stride. She lightly stroked that damp, warm brow.

"Aren't you going to look at me?" she said, and tried to make her voice calm.

"Of course, but you must light the candle first."

"It's morning, Sunniva. A brilliant day," said Tora sadly. "Look at me, please."

Those eyes, the vivid blue-gray eyes that could speak so clearly what she thought and felt, were completely inflamed. The film that covered each eyeball reminded Tora of the yolk of an egg.

She hadn't noticed the change! She had been too occupied with her wonderful discovery. She had forgotten to watch out for the leprosy in Sunniva. Meanwhile, it had managed to sneak up and take away her sight.

"No!" she screamed. "You can't lose your sight!"

"Don't cry!" snarled Sunniva. "I hate your crying for my sake. You know that. Can't you get it through your little head that I'm going to die?! No matter how many flowers you pick for me or how much food you steal, no matter how fine a time we have together. I will die."

She gasped for air and turned away.

Tora stood as if turned to stone.

"Pardon me," she said after a while. "I forgot myself."

"Yes, that you did," answered Sunniva. Her voice shook. "You know as well as I do that the dream of living on is the only dream that's forbidden. It just makes it impossible to bear the thought of death."

"I know. It won't happen again," whispered Tora. "May I do anything for you?"

"Yes," answered Sunniva softly. "You can please me by making particularly good progress. Now we have no time to waste, Tora. For I'll soon go to my reward. Then we'll both be free of debt. Won't that be fine?"

Tora smiled. "We seem to be alike," she said cautiously.

"Indeed, we may very well be," answered Sunniva quietly.

"But I don't despise myself as much as you do," said Tora.

She hadn't believed that she would ever dare say that. Perhaps it was their intimacy. Perhaps their certainty about the need for haste.

The room became deathly quiet.

Tora avoided looking at her. It was best to let her alone while she decided whether she would answer. She knew perfectly well what Tora meant.

Tora concentrated on forming the letters as nicely as she could on the little slate. For a long time the slate pencil's reluctant scraping was the only sound to be heard in the little bedroom.

Perhaps she had gone too far. But only time would tell. Now it was said, and she need never say that she knew about all the men who had paid with food and wine to be with Sunniva.

"You're a strange child," said Sunniva after a while.

In silence Tora let the slate pencil come to rest.

"Isn't there anything judgmental about you, or vindictive? Can you actually accept a person's being bad and good at the same time? Then you're truly more grown-up than I am."

There was nothing Tora could say now that would not ruin things. She had to let Sunniva finish with what she wanted to say.

"You know about the rest, too, don't you?"

"Yes."

"Would you tell me about it?"

"Do you really want me to?"

"Yes."

Tora looked at her for a long time.

Why should Sunniva want to hear her say what she herself had to know so extremely well? That she had hurt Tora both when she took the money and food in Tora's bundle and when she had sent that disgusting peasant to her. Did she want to ask for forgiveness, or did she just want to torture herself? Tora didn't know, but it suddenly didn't matter to her whether Sunniva said that she was sorry for what she had done.

"Not now," she said aloud. "We needn't think about it now."

"I need to say that I am sorry for all that I did to you. Can you forgive me?"

It was a prayer for mercy.

She is defenseless, thought Tora uneasily. We must be equal, or it won't work.

"I cannot forgive your taking my purse," she said severely. "My mother made it for me. It's my most beautiful remembrance."

"Yes, it is beautiful, and you should know that I have

taken good care of it. You'll find it in my chest. In the tray of the trunk."

Tora took a deep breath.

It was over. All the awful uncertainty was suddenly cleared up, dissolved into ordinary words. She felt empty. As if cleansed of the refuse of old sorrow and anger. There was nothing more left unsaid.

Tora rose and walked over to the chest. First she lifted the heavy lid, then the narrow cover of the tray. The embroidered purse lay on top, on a bed of fine lace. She held the purse between her hands for a long time.

"You know, it still has my mother's scent."

When she turned around, she looked right into Sunniva's eyes, and she knew that behind that yellow film of blindness the gaze was naked, bare of anger. There was only an aching left, the aching of a child who hasn't been allowed to cry enough.

Sunniva turned quickly toward the wall and lay there motionless. Tora sat down on the chair again and continued her laborious effort to draw letters that she knew could never be as beautiful as those she dreamed of.

It had grown completely dark in the room when she laid aside the slate pencil and the slate. She was tired and sad, but at the same time ecstatic and happy.

Sunniva moved. "Are you coming back tomorrow?" she mumbled at the wall.

"Of course."

"Would you read a particular book to me?"

"With pleasure."

"It will be difficult for you, since you'll have to read my mother tongue, which you don't understand. But it's my most precious book and the very last I want to hear. It means a great deal to me."

"With your help, I'll probably manage, don't you think?"

Tora bent over and touched the averted face with her lips.

She felt strangely confident and safe. It was a feeling that reminded her of how she had felt before Endre and she leaped across a dangerous gully.

14

ora quietly opened the door.

She hoped that Sunniva was sleeping, for she knew that the night had to have been extremely painful.

But she was awake.

"Come here, so I can feel the rain on the birch bough. I know you have been out to get it for me."

Tora laid the wet bough in her hands and watched as she brushed the twigs, with their tiny, fragrant leaves, across her face. Sunniva didn't say anything about the day before. They were completely finished with all that had so long remained unspoken. Tora was glad about that.

"I have something for you," said Sunniva suddenly. "You'll have to find it yourself. In the large chest, on the bottom, under my clothes. Hurry up! I can hardly wait to hear what you'll say."

Tora knelt down in front of the chest. Carefully she

lifted out the silk dresses, each one more brilliantly colored than the last. She knew that Sunniva had been beautiful before the leprosy. In those elegant clothes she must have resembled a fairy-tale princess.

"Now you've mastered the art of reading, Tora," said Sunniva ceremoniously. "You have earned your wings, and you are ready to fly wherever you wish in the world of books. My books are your treasure now, for the rest of your life."

"Do you really mean that?"

"It's no great sacrifice for me," said Sunniva calmly. "I can no longer read myself, and there is no one whom I would rather give them to than you."

Tora could scarcely believe her good fortune.

Only one thing had bothered her while she strove to learn to read. It was that she had no books to read. She had not dared to mention it to Sunniva, for it would sound as if she were begging to keep the Bible. After all that had happened, that was exactly what she couldn't bear Sunniva's thinking.

"Some of the books I'm particularly fond of. Do you want to know which they are or find your own favorite books to travel in?"

"I want to know which ones you like best."

"The books I never grow tired of are *Don Quixote*, *Gulliver's Travels*, and *The Journey of Niels Klim to the World Underground*. Three different books, written by very different authors, but when you have read them, I believe that you will perhaps think, as I do, that there are amazing similarities among the books. It's almost as if the authors were related, even though they are separated in time and by country."

"Tell me!" exclaimed Tora.

"No, do you think I want to rob you of the joy of discovering it all yourself?" she teasingly answered.

"Oh, how I am looking forward to it!"

"If you want to read to the other sick people and you need something edifying, I would recommend that you read from *The Soul's Sacrifice in Song,* which the virtuous Dorothea Engelbretsdatter wrote here in Bergen more than a hundred years ago. That will probably particularly please Marthe."

Tora remained kneeling before the chest, delighting in her great treasure of unknown worlds. Now she was certain that the time remaining to her would be entirely different from the way in which she had imagined it.

Without warning, spring, heavy with rain and filled with wind, passed into summer.

All at once the birch outside Sunniva's window was clad in luxuriant, thick foliage. The air streaming in through the window was mild and was strongly spiced by the scent of birch and sea. It carried with it laughter, shouts, and song, the sounds of wagon wheels creaking and horses' hooves busily clip-clopping across the cobblestones, gulls' sharp cries and thrushes' soft warbling.

That summer, which was so different from the summers she was used to at home, was filled with a strange, exciting liveliness. Tora was soon longing to feel the warm sea wind stroke her face and to see the summer unfold in that town below the tall mountains. But it was impossible now. She could no longer conceal her leprosy, and she could not stand the thought of being chased away. To go outside the hospital was impossible, but that did not lessen her longing.

It became increasingly difficult to concentrate on the book she was reading aloud to Sunniva. She didn't understand a word of the text, and she had to struggle to pronounce the words right and keep the rhythm of the verses. But she did her very best, for she saw how much it meant to Sunniva.

Suddenly time grew very short.

Sunniva was burning hot with fever the whole time, and her cough had become dry and rasping. It was not difficult to see that the little strength remaining to her was quickly disappearing.

Tora brought the Benefactor, but when he came, he only shook his head sorrowfully and whispered to Tora, "I would like to be alone with her awhile."

Tora sat outside the door in the dark and heard him talking for a long time. She could not hear if Sunniva was answering.

"Can I do anything for her?" she asked anxiously when he came out.

"You're already doing more than most have done her whole life," he answered. "But I know that you won't find peace until you have done everything in your power. If you come along down to my office, you can have some of our precious medicinal herbs. I hear you've learned to read? Then surely you'll also want to learn to make soothing potions for her, won't you?"

She could only nod.

It was good to have something else to think about when Sunniva fell asleep from exhaustion. Tora went down to the kitchen immediately. She made an extract from the leaves and seeds of agrimony, which eased coughing and soothed soreness in the chest. She had read that in the Benefactor's medical book. She boiled pearl barley in sharp vinegar and made red-hot porridge poultices, which she laid on Sunniva's chest several times a day. That would soothe the pain of the leprosy.

But she had to force Sunniva to drink agrimony tea, and she had to exert great effort in convincing Sunniva to let the poultices remain undisturbed on her chest. It was as if Sunniva had completely given up on her own body. As if she could no longer stand to be reminded of that painful prison. She mainly dozed now and had nearly stopped eating and drinking. She could no longer bear to be washed, but she smiled when Tora dampened her face with a cloth dipped in a mixture of vinegar and crushed elm leaves.

"Don't bother about my body," she said one day. "In any case, I am almost never present in it anymore. Just read more from *Paradiso,* so I can continue to dream of myself being where I long to be, floating freely beneath a cobalt-blue sky with stars of gold. Had there only been time, Tora, I would have told you a lot about Dante and *The Divine Comedy.* That powerful story is one I shall never grow tired of hearing. But we have no more time, Tora. I regret that."

"I'll always remember what you've told me," answered Tora quietly.

Before Tora had begun reading from *Paradiso* in a language she didn't understand, Sunniva had told about that great story which Dante had written nearly five hundred years before either of them had been born. It was Dante's journey through death, said Sunniva, from Hell to Purgatory to Paradise. She had described his experiences in Hell and Purgatory so vividly that Tora had seen them painfully clearly, and Sunniva stopped reciting.

"That's nothing for us to think about now," she had said. "We need Paradise and the happy account of Dante's reunion with his beloved Beatrice. She is the kind of woman I really like, the wise Beatrice, who shows Dante the whole divine order of creation, the visible and the invisible, the natural and the supernatural."

She fell silent.

Tora had long known that death was near, and she well remembered what she had promised Sunniva. Still, she began to cry hard. Death was coming all too soon. She was not prepared to lose so suddenly all that she had so recently found.

"You promised," said Sunniva weakly.

"I know, but I can't stand losing you yet, Sunniva. Not you, too."

Sunniva slowly turned her head toward her.

"Don't be greedy, Tora. You must understand that the price of love is its absence. Don't you think that I, too, feel its pain?"

She sounded almost angry.

"I who had protected myself so well, who was invulnerable for so long. I, who only wished that death would come quickly, have now begged death to wait. But time can't be stopped. We both know that. I must be allowed to leave, and you must guard your precious time. Use it in the world of books and you will have the happy ending that I promised you."

Sunniva grew quiet. For a very long time.

Tora listened intently for her breathing.

She regretted her outburst. It was inconsiderate of her

to wish that Sunniva should live longer. She knew how unbearable the pain had to be in a body where nothing worked any longer. Only the brain, voice, and hearing functioned, and it was with great difficulty that Sunniva stopped herself from screaming. It was greedy to wish for still more love. She had been given so much in such a short time. She had gotten a sister.

Still, she held her breath in fear that Sunniva would not reawaken. When Sunniva moaned in her sleep, she breathed more easily and continued silently to practice pronouncing words that to her were incomprehensible. She practiced with great intensity, for the last reading of the verses in that beautiful, singing language should be completed. As soon as Sunniva awakened, Tora began to read aloud, and she continued until she knew that Sunniva was far, far away.

Sunniva's waking moments became shorter and more painful. It was terrible to see how it tortured her to be back, and Tora began to wish that death would hurry.

Late one afternoon, Sunniva suddenly said, "Will you do something for me?" Her voice was more clear and calm than it had been in a long time.

"Of course." Tora glowed with joy.

"Will you comb my hair?"

Tora carefully lifted Sunniva's head and placed it on her lap.

With slow movements she let the brush glide through

Sunniva's thick, red-gold hair. For a long, long time, until it billowed and glowed like dark gold. It was strange that her hair was still just as heavy and shiny as before, completely untouched by leprosy, which otherwise had ravaged her body so terribly. Tora looked at her own hair. It, too, was as heavy and luxuriant as it had been before she became ill.

"Your hair is so beautiful."

"Yours, too," whispered Sunniva. "And we have the same color."

"I got the color of mine from my mother, did you know that?"

"And I got mine from my mother. She used to say that the most beautiful women in Italy have red hair. The most beautiful and the proudest, but not always the most honorable." She laughed weakly.

"Tell me about your mother," begged Tora.

"I'll tell you about spring in Florence and about Dante. Open the window wide, Tora. Let the twilight air fill the room. Summer's light and air in Bergen remind me so much of Mother's hometown, Florence. Perhaps it is the scent of a combination of sun-baked stones and damp green coolness, a sweet scent of expectation that you feel only at twilight. It was always at dusk that I sneaked out and wandered alone in the park, up the long lane of tall, cool poplars to the heights above the town. I could stand there for hours, enjoying the warm day's meeting with the cold of night, seeing the red tile roofs burning with dark light, and hearing the solemn church bells summoning everyone to Mass."

She chose her words with the greatest care and tied them together into sentences that glided into Tora's memory like a circle of slow-moving dancers.

During the long, gasping pauses, Tora continued combing.

"The doves, Tora, you should have seen the clouds of white doves that rose from the church domes at the first sonorous chime of the bells. I imagined that I was standing exactly where Dante must have stood thinking about *Divina commedia*, so many hundred years earlier. I felt certain that I knew why he didn't write in Latin, the language of the Church, but chose the language that ordinary people in Florence spoke. He probably wanted them to understand what he had to say about good and evil, about the lust for power and treachery, about a true love of God and hypocritical piety. I stood there and was filled with a furious triumph at having discovered that one of the Church's great men was not pure of heart, and I wished that I could do as Dante did. Write so people would remember and understand for a long, long time after I myself was gone . . ."

The words disappeared in a violent coughing fit. When it was over, Tora saw that Sunniva's breast was covered with a bloody froth.

Sunniva did not waken when Tora moistened her face and put a new porridge poultice on her.

Neither did she waken while Tora read from *Paradiso*. Tora continued reading until the candle burned out.

"Sleep in peace," she whispered.

Then she went out quietly and closed the door behind her.

15

ora had been getting Sunniva's burial vestment ready for a long time.

She had wanted to sew it herself, but not from that coarse cloth which came to the hospital in great rolls. Sunniva should be beautifully clad, Tora had decided. Like a bride.

She had not been able to tell Sunniva what she was planning. Tora knew, of course, that Sunniva didn't fear death at all or care what happened to her afterward. Still, it was too horrible to talk about. Only once had Tora been on the verge of revealing everything. It was on the day that Sunniva told her about the cemetery here in Bergen where her family plot lay and where her gravestone had already stood for a long time. She had said that it was a grieving angel in white marble. It was elegant and costly, of course, as was fitting for the deceased of her class. And even if she had not been present at her own burial, she knew that her father had spared no expense. The coffin had assuredly been costly, covered with white lilies and on an elegant wagon drawn by black horses. The wake had undoubtedly been lavish, with the whole family and the town's most prominent citizens present. They had surely grieved both long and deeply, she said, and laughed. But their sorrow was just as hollow as the casket was empty, for her father had long before buried Sunniva alive at the hospital. Naturally, under a false name, for it mustn't ever be known that loathsome leprosy had stricken the mighty shipyard owner's immediate family. There were already enough stories about his daughter.

It wasn't what Sunniva said but her tone that chilled Tora. Swept by gusts of inconceivable loneliness, Sunniva lived in hell on earth, and Tora couldn't comprehend that God could be so merciless as simply to let it happen. It was then that Tora felt, for the first time in her life, that she had to speak directly to Him. Late one evening she went into the church and knelt in front of the dark altar. She begged and implored, but no matter how often she asked, she received no answer. Then Tora decided that when Sunniva was laid to rest, she would be clad as the most beautiful of brides.

Tora searched among Sunniva's dresses for one that was really light and delicate. White or a rose-tinted silk would have been best, but she found nothing that was suitable. Most of Sunniva's dresses were in strong, daring colors. When dead, Sunniva shouldn't look like a fairy-tale princess. She should be clad as befitting one who was going wandering with the wise Beatrice.

There was enough fine white lace for the most beautiful veil any bride had ever had. Tora would make sure it resembled a veil made of the most delicate snow crystals.

The only thing she found that was fitting for Sunniva's vestment was the throw on the bed, that white woolen cloth which was a Garden of Eden, with its marvelous flowers, strange animals, and birds in all the colors of the rainbow.

While Tora had been caring for Sunniva, she had washed the throw many times. But she had never bothered to scrub it completely clean of blood and the pus of sores. Now she asked Marthe for help in beating it so clean that it was radiant. And Marthe was happy to help Tora, who had relieved her of the heavy duty of caring for Mistress Dybendal. Tora let Marthe believe that she wanted the throw for herself, and she did not protest when Marthe mumbled that, fortunately, they were rid of that awful witch.

After Sunniva died, Tora sat up the whole night sewing on the gown. She had cut it so that the bosom was covered by great bunches of pale red roses, while both sleeves were covered with yellow and blue butterflies.

She finished in the gray light of dawn. Then she walked out into the meadow behind the barn and picked an armful of dewy wildflowers. After that, she slowly began to wash Sunniva for the very last time. Her body was as light as a doll's, and her skin felt cool and dry.

As Tora dressed her, Marthe and Ranneveig came with

a coffin of raw planks. They quickly left again, without offering to help in laying Sunniva in the coffin. Perhaps they understood that Tora would rather look after her alone.

Tora placed a pillow beneath Sunniva's head and brushed her red hair until it formed a halo around her face. She covered Sunniva's face with a veil of fine lace and folded it extra tightly across the gaping hole of her mouth. She adorned Sunniva's hair with a wreath of daisies. In her hands Tora placed the rosary of crystal and ebony and a large bouquet of buttercups and bluebells. It completely hid the wrinkled, fingerless hands. Tora didn't want them to be visible in death.

Tora sat looking at her for a long time.

What a beautiful bride she was! One could almost believe that she was filled with anticipation.

The gown was cut exactly like the one Beatrice was wearing in the picture in the book. Tora took care to fold the cloth about the stumps of Sunniva's legs precisely as Beatrice's kirtle was folded when she was floating beside Dante toward the sun.

Tora was satisfied. She had done all she could in order for Sunniva's dream to be fulfilled. She would surely enjoy all eternity in her cobalt-blue heaven adorned with stars of gold.

Only Tora and the Benefactor accompanied Sunniva to a grave in the unkempt and overly filled cemetery behind the hospital. There, the most wretched were laid to rest:

the paupers, the hanged, and the many who had died of leprosy at the hospital.

It was a dreary, rainy day. The wind made it hard to carry the coffin, even though it was so light. The gravedigger waited impatiently by the open grave. As soon as the Benefactor was finished calling down God's peace on Sunniva, the gravedigger would begin to swing his shovel.

Earth to earth, ashes to ashes, dust to dust.

The Benefactor's voice was calm and sincere, as if he were wishing her a good journey. He seemed to notice neither the rain nor the gravedigger's impatient glances. He slowly sprinkled the black soil across the coffin lid. Then he leaned over and dropped a white lily on the soil.

"You deserve a reward for your great kindness, Tora," he said as they walked back to the hospital. "She received a dignified end to her tragic life, thanks to you. I know that you felt more than benevolence toward her. I want you to know that I, too, respected her, despite our deep disagreement and all her sinful ways. Seldom have I met a person so rejected and ill-used by everyone and so fervently scorned by herself. But neither have I seen such courage and endurance as hers."

Tora stared mutely at her soiled clogs. The ice-cold mud made her feet ache maddeningly.

She would have liked to tell him everything, but she knew that her voice wasn't to be trusted. Sunniva's absence was like an open wound. When she again could manage to speak calmly, she would ask the Benefactor to see to it that she was buried beside Sunniva.

She sat on Sunniva's chair and stared out at the rain. It didn't stop raining until late into the evening. She waited until it was nighttime and quiet before she crept through the hospital gate. She had put on Sunniva's black velvet cape, which completely covered her body and head. If she met a late wanderer in the night or a watchman, she probably wouldn't be stopped. The sight of that costly cape would surely keep everyone at a respectful distance.

It had not been difficult to figure out how to get to the exclusive cemetery. Marthe had talked incessantly about the difference, even in death, between wealthy and poor. She had described exactly where the cemetery lay, the one with the great weeping willows and the many costly monuments.

There was not a soul to be seen beyond the hospital gate. Apart from the cats, the usually busy Division Street was completely abandoned. Large cats, small cats, thin and fat, brindled and velvet black—all rushed around on their nightly hunt for rats and bats without paying her any heed.

The moon shone white and transparent against the pale-green sky. Tora breathed in the damp night air in deep drafts. There was a wonderful fragrance, spiced by sea and tar, burned wood and flowers.

Flowers. She wanted to bring flowers along. The apothecary's garden was the town's finest, that she knew.

Marthe had said so. The garden was open to the public and Marthe was wont to go there when she needed something beautiful to look at.

Even protected by black velvet and darkness in the narrow passages, Tora felt her heart hammering with terror as she walked along. She breathed a sigh of relief in front of the garden gate. It was standing ajar. It was dark in the tunnel of linden trees, but behind the pitch darkness she could glimpse the shining silver surface of a little lake, Lille Lunggårdsvann. Tora had taken off her clogs. Her steps mustn't be heard on the gravel. Pains flashed at every careful step, but she couldn't risk being stopped now.

Never had she seen the like of such floral splendor. It was as if Sunniva's coverlet with its Garden of Eden had come alive. The beds were bulging with lush leaves and the great crowns of flowers. The fragrance was overwhelming and changed from heavy and sweet to light and spicy. She knew that those plants and flowers were rare and valuable, for many of the Swan Apothecary's medicinal herbs were grown here.

She shivered with a mixture of joy and fear. It was wrong to steal. Of course it was wrong! But Sunniva was going to have the very very best. She would willingly become a thief for her sake. For Tora had decided that someone should learn that Sunniva was loved and not forgotten. Someone should be made to feel ashamed of having betrayed her.

She chose painstakingly. Five white lilies from one bed, five hollyhocks from another, a branch of yellow-white roses from one rose tree, and a branch of deep-red roses from a bush farther on. It could scarcely be seen that she had picked anything from that abundance. She had quite certainly done no harm.

All at once she heard that she was humming. It was a long time since she had done that! Indeed, she was happy just now. Alone in the middle of the night in the Garden of Eden as she picked the very finest bouquet for her Sunniva.

At the shore of the lake she suddenly stopped.

The sight of rich buttercups glittering along the moonlit lake left her nearly breathless. She remembered them just like that, large as globeflowers. She could still feel the brownish-black marsh water trickling up between her toes, the lush grass stroking her legs as she stretched out for the large buttercups while trying to avoid the spray from the thundering rapids.

The bouquet had grown much larger than she had planned, but she still managed to hide it beneath the black cape while she walked up the hill toward the cemetery. It was very hard to breathe, and pain hammered in her legs. But now she could see the gate. Behind it she saw, just as Marthe had described them, the tombstones and monuments of the well-to-do who had died.

There was a solemnity in here. Foreign and dismissive.

She shivered. Could it be the enormous trees that gave her the feeling of being a trespasser? The poplars resembled well-kempt, black-clad watchmen. The weeping willows, with their branch skirts whispering against the ground, reminded her of strict old women. In the deep shade beneath the copper beeches, it seemed as if eyes were silently watching her.

Tora suddenly wished she were invisible, that she could escape from feeling the dead glances of the polished angels of marble and granite. There were a great many angels here, sitting, standing, or leaning over the graves.

She began to search for Sunniva's sorrowful angel. It took time before she found it, since she had not quite understood what Sunniva had meant when she talked about the family plot. She had to read the names on the graves to find the right angel. When at last she found it, she remained standing there, just staring, for a long time. Sunniva's angel stood leaning against a colossus of marble that resembled a gloomy, fairy-tale castle.

With a sorrowful little smile, the angel stared down at the marble slab bearing Sunniva's real name.

"If you really are her guardian angel, you will rejoice in this," whispered Tora.

She arranged the roses and the lilies prettily on the topmost part of the marble slab, and she laid the buttercups in the angel's arms. It looked just as if the angel had closed its hands around the bouquet.

Tora saw immediately that it was not possible to remove the false date of Sunniva's death. It was carved deep into the marble.

She had suspected that beforehand.

Actually, it didn't matter all that much. They were going to understand anyway.

She took out the sheet of slate she had found at the hospital. She had polished and rubbed it until it shone like silver. The sheet of slate had been easy to scratch, and she had not made any mistakes, even though there were many words:

Be Loved for All Eternity, Sunniva
Who Expired in the Year of Our Lord
1813 from Cruel
Leprosy at St. Jørgen's Hospital
in Bergen
Float in Your Golden Heaven

She pressed the soil around the slate sheet and supported it well with beautiful stones that she brought from the graves of other members of Sunniva's family.

Would anyone dare to remove it?

She didn't think so!

The angel smiled crookedly at her as she left.

HOMECOMING

16

verything was changed after Sunniva died. Tora sat in the little bedroom with the empty bed. She felt numb and hollow. She didn't have the strength to eat, and she couldn't sleep. She could think of nothing but absence. It was as if she herself no longer existed. White days and nights glided into one another, and she no longer knew what was real. She tried to think of the time before the hospital, but it was unreal, too, like a sun-filled dream of a girl who ran barefoot through the grass. A girl who didn't understand she was living the only, precious life she had.

She stared at the hourglass that she had placed on the windowsill. The top globe was empty. In the bottom globe, time lay completely immobile in thousands of shining grains of sand. If she turned the hourglass, time would begin to run again. Quietly, nearly unnoticeably, the glass would be filled by moving time. If she wanted it to be. But she didn't, for time went only forward and it was back that she wanted to go. Back to the time before she knew that life was once and for all and that it could never be lived over again.

Her pain was terribly real. It slashed beneath her skin. Slashed and slashed body and soul; she didn't know where one pain started and the other stopped.

"The torments of the soul are the worst," Sunniva had said. "The pains of the body you can sometimes deaden or nearly learn to live with, but not the pains of the soul. They are never eased. The soul's wounds are always open."

At that time Tora had no notion what sorrow of the soul was. Now she knew, and it had changed everything.

The empty bed and the books that she had sorted into stacks were real, as was the figure with the glorious shining hair. One who quickly turned her back on her when she began to cry, who hissed at her with a voice that no longer existed:

You are an idiot! Why are you wasting your time searching for me, when you have so little time to find yourself?

"But I don't want to be me. I want to be you. I want to be where you are!"

But you can't be, silly little girl! You can never in all eternity be like me, for you haven't lived or thought as I have. You know but a little part of me, and you can't imagine my loneliness. Stop wishing that you were me. Stop mulling over what is actually real. You'll get nowhere with it anyway. Every-

thing you have experienced earlier is no longer real. It was once, but it isn't now. What has been could just as well have been a dream, isn't that so? Perhaps your being here is a bad dream. Have you thought about that?

"It's no dream that you are dead and that I shall soon die," she shouted.

The sound of her voice was frightening in the quiet room.

I am just saying that it could have been a dream! Did you understand nothing when we were together? Have you still not understood that I taught you to read so that you would find meaning in your life? You were an ignorant child when you were marked by death. When we met, you used all your precious time toiling for others and brooding over your illness. You had nothing more than hopelessness to look forward to. But now you have mastered the art of reading, and you yourself can change the tiny bit that remains of your life. Don't you see that you can dream the most fantastic dreams? Hurry, Tora! Read before it is too late. Read and find out what you think. Then you will understand that what you think and believe is what you are.

She wanted to say that she was sorry, but she knew that the gossamer figure wouldn't care for that.

Carefully Tora tried to rise from the chair. It took very little now to awaken the most terrible pains in her feet. If she stepped down on her right foot with all her weight, she would certainly faint. It had happened several times while she was clearing away Sunniva's books. But if she really stretched, she could just reach the topmost book on the stack nearest the chair. Then she didn't have to bother her feet.

"Look forward to traveling in the most amazing worlds," Sunniva had once said.

"But is what's written in the books really true?" Tora had asked.

"Is that so important? It's not easy to say what is true or not true, for the world is endlessly large and time is inconceivably much older than we are. Our lives are just specks of dust in the whole: what has been, what is, and what is coming after us. We can never be quite certain that what we are experiencing is completely true, is just partially true, or is a lie and foolishness," Sunniva had answered. "You'll have to get used to it, my simple, gullible friend. But I hope that you'll find your utopia in books and get to experience all that life has denied you."

"Utopia, what is that?"

"It's the Land of Nowhere or Everywhere. It's the world as you would like it to be. Seek in the books, then you'll surely find it."

The book that now lay in her lap was *The Journey of Niels Klim to the World Underground*. It was thick and heavy and secretive.

She suddenly realized that she was hungry. For the first time in ages. She wondered if Marthe was coming soon with the food. It had to be a long time since she last came. Whether it was yesterday or today that Marthe had discreetly knocked and asked if she would have soup, Tora didn't know, for the days had blended together. But the next time Marthe knocked, she would not shout, "Leave me in peace." She would say loudly, "Come in here to me, Marthe."

In the hourglass, time was waiting. It shone like thousands of tiny little stars.

This was the first book she was going to read just for her own sake. The feeling this brought was simultaneously solemn and frightening, as if, all on her own, she was going to begin a journey toward an unknown destination. It had to be done right, she thought. The book had to be read as the author had intended from the first to the last page.

Sunniva had said that books deserved to be read with patience.

She speculated for a while about whether it was better to read silently or aloud. After a while she decided that she wanted to hear her own voice, for perhaps Sunniva would also hear it, someplace in her cobalt-blue heaven.

For a long time she studied the book without opening it.

The cover with its gold pattern of twisting leaves was

beautiful. With her fingertips she could feel how deeply the letters were imprinted into the leather. This book was a costly treasure. She wanted to enjoy every single letter.

She opened the book and read aloud:

THE JOURNEY OF NIELS KLIM TO THE WORLD UNDER-GROUND, BY LUDVIG HOLBERG. TRANSLATED FROM THE LATIN ORIGINAL, NICOLAI KLIMII ITER SUBTERRANEUM, BY JENS BAGGESEN, COPENHAGEN, 1789.

Holberg must have been a learned man, since he wrote in Latin, for that was the Church's and the scholars' language. Sunniva had said so. She had also been able to read and write Latin, but Tora didn't know why Sunniva had learned a language that no ordinary people spoke.

As she read the table of contents, she thought that each chapter title was like a door ajar. Behind the doors were the most peculiar occurrences. Perhaps also unpleasant, but it no longer seemed so frightening that she would meet the unknown entirely by herself. She hadn't believed that she would ever feel curiosity again. Now she discovered that she was impatient to know what was concealed behind "The Author's Arrival on the Planet Nazar," "The Journey to the Firmament," or "The Voyage to the Lands of Wonder." The mysterious words drove her to read quickly on.

"The Author Becomes Monarch Underground." So had he perhaps found his utopia? But, sorry to say, his good fortune didn't last long. That she understood from the title of the next chapter: "A Sudden Change in Fortune." And it seemed that things got even worse, for the last chapter was called "The Author's Return to His Fatherland and the End of the Fifth Monarchy."

Something terribly serious must have happened. Whatever it was, she would surely find out if she read just a little of the last chapter; then she wouldn't have to worry through the whole book. No, she had promised to read the way the author had intended that the book should be read, from beginning to end. She would have to rein in her impatience. But she could look at the pictures. They told a story, too.

The first picture showed Niels Klim falling through the earth with a terrified expression on his face. It was easy to imagine what he was feeling as he floated with only open air above and below him. Just as she herself had felt so many times when she and Endre leaped across the rapids, a mixture of terror and delight.

The next picture showed Neils Klim asleep on a stone, while a large ox stood looking at him. The ox didn't seem threatening; it seemed rather as if it was wondering what the man was doing there. In the background she saw a shadowy figure. She couldn't see the figure's legs, but its arms were clearly drawn. They were outstretched, as if to bid Niels Klim welcome.

In the next picture Niels Klim had raised his arm in

greeting before the strangest beings Tora had ever seen. They had feet like roots and arms like branches and faces like those of human beings. That they were people of high rank she understood immediately, for Niels Klim seemed extremely respectful. Whoever could they be? What were they talking about? Maybe Niels Klim was telling them about his hometown with its seven mountain peaks and high, open sky? It was certainly not easy to see from the picture whether their conversation was peaceful or antagonistic.

She quickly turned the pages to the next picture and then the next. All the pictures were simultaneously meaningful and mysterious and made her even more curious about what the words were concealing.

She would soon have to read the story itself, she thought, nearly irritated! She would obtain answers to the questions tumbling around in her head.

Only then did she realize how warm she had become and how fast her heart was beating.

She leaned back in the chair, amazed.

Something strange had happened to her. She felt wide-awake and as rested as after a long, deep sleep. A good feeling of desire and impatience began in her stomach and spread out to her whole body and made her feel light and strong. Like a hawk just before it took to its wings.

She was alive again.

Here in this narrow bedroom she was free, was with

Niels Klim on a journey to the unknown. It would also be her journey.

Sunniva was not far away, after all, for the book was filled with evidence of her having read it. Here and there she had written short exclamations in the margins, underlined a word or a sentence, or marked off a whole chapter. Tora understood that Sunniva had been particularly occupied with the chapters called "On Nature in the Land of Potus" and "The People's Way of Thinking" and "On the Religion of the Potuan Nation." Tora looked forward to finding out why.

Do you understand what I mean?

"Yes," she answered aloud to the voice in her head. "Now I understand what you have given me."

Then you'll be able to manage for yourself after this.

"I can manage for myself, but surely you aren't going to leave me?

No, never entirely. But I have other things to do than to be your mother hen. You understand that, don't you? Read Niels Klim *and* Don Quixote *and* Gulliver's Travels *and enjoy them slowly, little sparrow. And you must read the foreword to* Niels Klim's *account carefully, even though it is difficult to grasp for you who know so little about humankind's lust for power, but it's about what you so much want to know.*

"About what?"

About reality and dream. About what truth actually is.

"Wait! Explain to me . . ."

No! You must learn to explain for yourself!

She read "An Apologetic Preface, Peder Klim and Andreas Klim, Sons of Thomas Klim and Grandsons of Klim the Great, to the Benevolent Reader" and became alarmed at its difficult words and indignant tone. But she could understand that it was necessary to assure the reader that the journey underground wasn't a lie and fantasy. For she herself was, of course, someone who doubted everything she hadn't seen with her own eyes. Conscientiously she read the testimonies of "Men Whose Honesty and Sincerity was Above all Suspicion." But she was not really interested in the author's defense of Klim's credibility until she came to the testimony of that strange man Peyvis. He had come to Bergen from distant Finmark, where there were to be found people who with natural magic could transform themselves into wolves, speak completely unknown languages, or travel from the South Pole to the North Pole in less than an hour. Tora had never heard of anything stranger. It was magic that Endre would have liked.

In Bergen the town judge had ordered Peyvis to concentrate all his powers of wizardry on taking a journey under the earth. It must have been a frightful sight when Peyvis transformed himself into an eagle that disappeared into the air. Not until a month later had the quite exhausted Peyvis popped up in the judge's drawing room. It was on a Friday morning, just before sunrise. He described his voyage through the air and his trip through the lands beneath the earth and reported that Niels Klim's son, under the name Niels the Second, was ruling far and wide over the world beneath the earth. Everything he told was penned, word for word, by learned men.

That happened a long time ago here in Bergen. It was scarcely to be believed, but even if it was strange, it wasn't necessarily a lie, thought Tora. Was that what Sunniva had wanted her to understand? That there was truth that sounded like a lie and lies that sounded like the truth and that not all that was to be found between heaven and earth could be explained?

It was easier to accept than she had believed, and finally, she could begin to read. Finally, she would find out exactly how Niels Klim found his way to the inside of the earth. Finally!

Soon she was captured by Niels Klim's unique experiences in a land where trees spoke as people do, just many times more wisely and nobly than she herself had heard people speak. So enthralled was she that she paid no heed to the hours that passed, the darkness that gathered, and the hunger that made her stomach hurt. She just barely noticed that there was a loud knocking at the door.

"Come in, Marthe," called Tora.

"I thought I heard voices," said Marthe. She glanced suspiciously around the room. "I thought you were alone."

She had soup with her, Tora saw. And a thick slice of

bread. It was long since she had tasted bread. Hunger made her mouth water.

"I am alone, but I'm reading aloud to myself."

"Yes, of course," said Marthe, still suspicious. "You are reading the highborn Mistress's books, apparently."

"I'm glad you've come, Marthe," Tora hurried to say. "I need you so."

"Do you?" Marthe melted at once. "I have saved the best of the soup for you today. It's so thick with grain that you can chew it. You have to get some fat on those thin legs of yours, little bird."

"Thanks, Marthe."

Marthe busied herself with clearing a place for the food on the little table.

While Tora ate, Marthe told about all that had happened at the hospital in the last few days. New patients had come, but several had also died, mainly older people. All in all, there were no additional mouths to feed. She sighed.

Tora had known several of the old people well. But the worst was to learn that the young peasant woman was dead, she who had seemed so strong. Tora remembered when she had come to the hospital, newly married and pregnant with her first child. She had consoled her spouse, who had followed her in and couldn't bear to leave her. Tora had heard him crying outside the gate for a long time before he walked away. The young peasant woman was just as frightened as all the others who came to the hospital, but she didn't give in to anguish and self-pity. She used her time to talk to, and care for, the old people, and then she sang for her unborn child. Hummed and sang and stroked her round stomach, as if she were promising the child everything that was good in this world. Now she was dead, just before she was to bear the child. Her name was Sara. It was unusually beautiful, like the name of a flower.

"How did she die?"

"Choked to death."

Tora grew cold. The worst death of all.

"And the child?"

"It died along with her, thank God," said Marthe. "Well, you know how it is, Tora. There is no future for anyone here."

"How are things going now?" Tora asked hesitantly, frightened to hear the answer.

"As before, just a little worse. There has been much too little of everything for so terribly long. Hunger and disease tear people away the whole time, and now that Ranneveig has taken to her sickbed, the dirt is up to my ears. I don't think she can bear being here any longer. Neither can anyone else, it looks like. We get no help. Nor is there any money to pay anyone, and it seems as if the people in town have lost their senses in their terror of the hospital. You'd think it was Satan's house, the way they act. But the truth is that you won't find any people more pious in the whole town of Bergen than precisely those here at the hospital."

Tora saw that Marthe had become stooped.

Strong, staunch Marthe with her steadfast belief in God's mercy suddenly seemed little and helpless. Poor Marthe. Perhaps she was beginning to lose hope that God was listening.

But suddenly she straightened her back and smiled at Tora. Her old confident smile.

"Here we sit talking as if you had been away for a long time, and it is only seven days since the Mistress's burial."

"Is it really no longer than that?"

"No. But I know that it has been much longer for you."

"I have been to a place where time doesn't count," answered Tora quietly.

"But you're back now?"

"Yes, now I'm back." She smiled. "No, that isn't completely true. For now I'm in the world of books, Marthe. Oh, you can't believe how fantastic it is there! Did you know, for example, that Niels Klim, who lived here in Bergen many years ago, discovered a cave in a mountain, Ulrikken-fjellet, one day when he was climbing there? And before he had any idea what was happening, he was falling, through Ulrik Mountain, all the way down to a land where trees were people who talked and thought and acted in an entirely different way than we do, and . . ."

"Never heard the like! Did he come to the netherworld?" said Marthe, alarmed.

"No, not to the elfin folk or the usual netherworld beings. It's not about sprites or ghosts."

Tora stopped. She didn't know how she should explain what was so different about the Potuans.

"I love stories." Marthe smiled. "I can see that you do, too, sweet child. You have roses in your cheeks. Those you haven't had for as long as I've known you."

"I feel . . . fine," said Tora. "Actually fine."

She meant it sincerely.

Marthe leaned over and stroked her cheek. "I see that. Now I would like to ask if you are going to sit up here entirely alone for all eternity, or are you going to come down to the rest of us?"

Tora hesitated in answering. Everything *was* changed. She herself as well. Perhaps she was so changed that it would be difficult to be together with the others again. Perhaps she would lose her newly won freedom if she again had to share her room with others' fear and pain. In the silence here she could dream and wait for Sunniva.

"Won't you come down and share with the rest of us?"

"What do you mean?"

"I mean that you have mourned long enough," said Marthe firmly. "Besides, if you come down to the hall again, you can do those you are living here with a great deal of good."

"But I can't help anyone any longer," protested Tora. "I can't tend or wash them or carry food. You know I can scarcely walk."

"Yes, I know," said Marthe. "And I can see that you

need to have the sores on your feet tended to. But the others need you. You can read to them. You can help them to get away for a time from the hunger and the death and the hate out in town."

"Yes, I can. I want to."

Marthe carried the beautiful chair down and placed it in front of the tall, narrow windows in the hall where the light lasted the longest. She also took along the table and the candlestick and the hourglass and all the books. And last she carried Tora down and noticed sadly how light she had become.

17

ora sat on the chair by the window and began to read. At first so softly that she could scarcely hear her own voice, then louder, when she noticed that it grew silent at the table and that the faces turned, listening, toward her. She read the whole day and stopped only while people were preparing supper for themselves out in the kitchen and carrying it in to the table to eat.

After the evening prayer, she began to read again.

Then she saw that the flock of children had gathered close around her chair. As the light disappeared and Niels Klim told about "The Potuans' Constitution," Tora felt a warm pressure against her knee. A little girl was sleeping with her head leaning against her. In the girl's arms an even younger girl slept just as soundly. They resembled angels with their shining tow-colored hair and transparent skin. Both had the same sprinkling of tiny rose-colored freckles on their arms and legs, and Tora realized that they were sisters who had only each other. She read on quietly and was astonished that she had not before noticed how beautiful these two were.

Tora read aloud every day.

She read while the light summer darkened into a rain-filled autumn, and the weeks were filled with pale mist and torrential rain, which lasted until the icy cold set in. While the cold collected as frost on the inside walls and crept under one's skin, Tora read about green meadows that steamed with heat and luxuriant woods where the rain tasted as sweet as honey.

The cold held the town and its people captive for many discouraging weeks, but Tora read about deserts and beaches so hot that they burned the soles of one's feet, and the breathless silence in the hall told her that they all felt the heat, no matter how cold it was around them.

Eventually the grip of the cold was loosened, and soft, heavy snowflakes began to fall. The snow sifted quietly down for days and nights and covered the mountains and the town with a thick white blanket. Soft snowdrifts grew and grew around the hospital and sheltered cracked walls and frozen souls.

The snow warmed, but it could not still hunger.

Whether poor crops and bad fishing were the cause of the hospital's scarcely receiving any alms this stormy winter, no one knew. But everyone knew that a terrible time was approaching. Marthe was desperately worried about the sick. Her ingenuity in her search for food was endless. She begged for fish entrails at the wharf and cut the bark from trees and boiled soup of all the plants that were edible. But hunger still roamed like a ghost through the hospital, each day harvesting its dead.

Tora couldn't help Marthe in curbing hunger, but she could read. And she read more fervently than ever before, read the most beautiful stories she could find. Luckily Sunniva had loved books that dealt with fantastic lands and realms where peace and mercy ruled, where food was to be found in abundance, where trees were heavy with ripe fruit and the heads of grain grew as large as fists and fat and shiny fish swam right up into the nets.

Dreams filled no one, she knew. But they made existence less intolerable for the most wretched in Bergen during that time. They were to learn that there were many others who were hard hit. More and more often the recently widowed, old men, and orphaned children came to the hospital to ask for shelter and protection. As often as the Benefactor thought he could, he received them, for it was at odds with his conscience not to be merciful. But Tora understood that he felt it bitterly ironic that no other doors were open to the wretched than the gate to the detested hospital, where privation was already hopelessly immense.

Tora stared out the window at the heavy snowflakes that floated down thickly and silently.

In the rays from the powerless afternoon sun the snow-drifts glittered with a singularly intense brightness. It was as if the firmament had sent all its stars as a mild consolation to all those in need.

It was Christmas Eve and quiet in the hospital.

An odd expectation reigned. Everyone shared the same fragile hope that something wonderful was going to happen. Everyone feared one more disappointment.

After months of reading, Tora's eyes were tired and her throat was sore, but she felt satisfied with her work. For to people who otherwise felt only hopelessness, she had given dreams to console themselves with. Now she wondered what she could give them on this joyous day when they were going to celebrate the birth of Jesus Christ.

She knew that the Benefactor would give them the most beautiful Christmas church service he could. But afterward there would not be much food in their bowls for feasting and scarcely a splash of beer in their mugs. Even if Marthe had hidden away some logs of wood for the stoves and some extra candles for the long table in the hall in order to create a festive atmosphere, it would not be enough to prevent them all from feeling forsaken by the world.

What should she do?

She wanted so much to surprise them, enthrall them, see their eyes shine with excitement and joy. But at the same time she was afraid of offending the most pious if she read a story that was too lively. On a day like this she wouldn't dream of causing discord. While she was reading *Niels Klim,* there had been enough sulking and angry remarks, particularly from the old woman from Arna with whom she was sharing a room. As ill as the woman was, she still had strength enough to scold most people for trivialities. And Tora received a rebuke for her reading.

Tora decided to ask the Benefactor's advice.

"A singular problem, my child." He smiled. "But I do understand you all too well," he hurried to add. "You are surely right that it would be appropriate to read from the pious Dorothea Engelbretsdatter's *The Soul's Sacrifice in Song* or *Sacrifice of Tears.* They are edifying and beautiful songs on sin and atonement, the light of mercy, and a preparation for death. But most people here know the prayers for forgiveness of sin all too well. On a joyous day like this, they probably are most in need of being astonished and surprised. If you are asking what I would most like to hear, you have my answer: something wonderful, something unexpected."

"Do you mean like *Don Quixote de la Mancha?*" asked Tora hopefully.

"Precisely! I myself would like to hear some of the remarkable adventures that the famous Don Quixote experienced on his many journeys. Maybe if I got to battle side by side with Don Quixote against all the world's wrongs, it would make me forget my worry about all of you for a short time."

"Then you will stay and listen while I read?"

"Yes, I would very much like to stay."

"But what about your family?" Tora ventured to ask. She knew his child was precious to him. She knew, too, that his love was reciprocated. She had seen that when little Johan Sebastian accompanied his father on his hospital rounds.

He smiled. "My family knows that I'm in good company. Besides, it can be inspiring to hear about Don Quixote's battle against the windmills before I must go home to continue my own battle to awaken the consciences of our highest officials to the lepers' cause."

While the snowflakes continued, by the grace of God, to drift down like shining stars and the candles slowly burned, Tora read from that book which she herself had so long looked forward to beginning.

The flock of children sat closely around the chair as usual. The angelically beautiful sisters, Agnes and Kristin, had taken their customary places between her knees. They couldn't be budged, and Tora liked having them there. Their trusting warmth did her good.

The great, cold hall was transformed into a strange sun-filled landscape with towns and palaces that no one had ever seen but could all vividly imagine. They held their breath with excitement when the unconquerable knight Don Quixote rode out on his thin nag, Rosinante, to meet all kinds of danger followed by the worried Sancho Panza on his tired donkey. They chuckled at Sancho's sensible conversations with his lord and master and shook their heads over the people at the inn who had fun at the expense of the unfortunate knight.

It was long past midnight when Tora closed the book.

"You have given us all a marvelous Christmas Eve," said the Benefactor. "Now I'll return strengthened to my *Description of the Lepers in St. Jørgen's Hospital.* The night won't seem so long after this evening, and the battle against my windmills doesn't seem quite so hopeless."

She saw that around the long table they were also satisfied. As if they felt their hunger stilled. Many, both the younger and the older, came over to take her hand in thanks for the reading. That had not happened before.

All at once she felt how rich she was. It was almost as if she possessed a magic power that could transform darkness to light for a little while.

"I'm proud of you," whispered Marthe.

She had come to carry Agnes and Kristin to bed. They had long since fallen asleep in Tora's lap with their arms around each other.

"And I'm happy that you brought me back. Marthe, where are the little girls going to sleep tonight?"

"On the kitchen floor. I've put a sort of mattress in one corner for them. Then we'll see whether we can find a better solution later. It's not so easy, since they are not patients. Just orphans and deserted children of the poor."

"They can have my bed," said Tora.

"No, that's too much. You've just now gotten your own bed in the room for the first time," protested Marthe.

"But actually I like it on the floor between the beds. That's what I'm most used to," answered Tora. "Besides, I think they need me."

She gently touched the small heads in her lap. Their tow-colored shocks of curly hair felt soft and warm as down. "And I most probably need them."

18

*he white disk of the sun saw her, everything saw her and knew that she was there, only he did not. He did not know that she was there to be seen by him and only him.*

Night after night the memory returned.

Came and supplanted all the fantastic stories she had filled her thoughts with before she fell asleep and turned her over to the dream in which she was always doubly present— was always both Tora when little and Tora now, who tried to convince little Tora to do things differently from the way she had. But the attempts were in vain, and she was always helplessly present as the same painful events took place.

Night after night.

It had been a wonderful summer day.

One of those white days when the vault of the sky is

like highly polished silver. She couldn't look at the sun, but she knew that it was nearly dissolved in its own dazzlingly white heat. And she knew that the sun saw her, just as the flowers and trees saw her, as she leaped along the winding brook, down across the mountain, toward the road on the floor of the valley, where she would wait to meet him.

"Just wait, then you'll see," she shouted confidently to everything, and all things waited. The birch refrained from rustling its sun-dried leaves, the butterflies sat motionlessly on the foxgloves, and the grass refused to bow before the wind. Not even the black shadows dared to creep across the white cart tracks.

"Just wait, you'll soon see!" she mumbled to the flowers hanging limply in her warm hand. Everything was quiet, nothing changed. The dry earth burned beneath her bare feet. Her hand was tired from shielding her eyes against the white bend in the road where she would first see him. She had to let her hand fall and her tears flow freely from her squinting eyes. Just a little longer now. He would soon come, for she had waited so long. Quickly she turned her glance toward the shadow beneath the trees and bathed her sun-blinded eyes in that cool darkness, so they could again stand the strong midday light. She was tired, hungry, and thirsty, but she mustn't let the road out of her sight. If she looked away just a moment too long, the enchantment could be broken. Then he would not see her. Not this time either.

She heard his voice before she saw him coming around

the bend. Disappointed, she understood that he was not alone. Right away she knew that it was useless, for he would be busy with the stranger. No one in the world was as friendly and attentive to visitors as he was.

She wanted to call and wave, but her dried tongue clove to the roof of her mouth, and her hands refused to rise up. She stood there like that, mute and still, as he approached, and she heard him say, "That's my youngest daughter there, the straggler," before he turned toward her and said severely, "What are you doing down here in the valley? Does your mother know about this?"

Then he had looked right at her, but through her, and she couldn't make herself say that it was her birthday and that all she wanted was to hold his hand going up along the winding brook and to be the first who got to hear about everything he had done out there in the world, away from all that she was familiar with.

He continued on past her, and he and the stranger laughed confidentially.

"Don't look at me anymore!" she had whispered to the sky before she threw the withered flowers into the brook.

Tora awakened each morning and knew that she had cried in her sleep. The echo stayed with her the whole day.

Why did this memory come back now? After all, she had buried it so deeply. She had stopped worrying over why she was invisible to him long ago. Even her sorrow, she had long since grown out of.

She didn't want it to be like that now. She needed all her days to be clean and clear, without the shadows of childhood's defeats. If only she could force it to fade, as all memories of her life before the hospital had faded into unreal dreams she didn't miss. But for all her striving to oust the memory, she still heard a girl's reedy voice pleading: *Look at me, please.*

Something had called the memory up.

She knew what it was. The diary that contained the key to Sunniva's life. She had read it without suspecting that Sunniva's account would touch her own life and evoke memories she believed were long forgotten.

For a long time she had not been able to look at the diary without seeing Sunniva's dead face. It took equally long before she could bear to start reading that elegant handwriting. Still, after so much time had passed, she heard Sunniva's calm, cool voice behind the writing. Clearly, as if she were in the room and were speaking.

Sunniva had written about her life, but it was really her father she told about. Her wealthy and mighty father who, after his first, childless marriage, had brought Sunniva's mother, that young, spirited, red-haired beauty, from Italy. In Bergen she was very poorly received by the father's family, because she was young and beautiful and was taking the place of an extremely pious woman who had died all too early; because she was well-read and musical and her temperament was foreign; but in particular because she refused to give up her Catholic faith. In spite of all the children she gave him, she remained exiled and lonely. Long years of cold and isolation from the Bergensian bourgeoisie was a slow-working poison that disturbed her mind and weakened her health. She had not herself chosen to travel to the cloister in Fiesole outside Florence, but when Sunniva's father decided that she should go, she asked only that Sunniva might accompany her. He had not been against that. On the contrary, he hurried to find cheap passage on the ship to Genoa. Like the good merchant he was, he wanted to finish with this unfortunate business as quickly as possible.

The text changed quite surprisingly. It was equally well formulated, but its preoccupied tone was gone:

I cannot actually remember a single touch, never a pat on the head or a squeeze of the hand in broad daylight. My father was quite simply not made in such a way that he could show a feeling that he had not previously reckoned the value of. As a child it hurt me deeply that I was never worthy of a glance or a caress in public. I could only understand it as loathing, and I was ashamed of being unimportant, a nonentity in his life. How I made myself miserable with worry over what I had done wrong! How I strove to attain his praise! I felt like a pup wagging its tail, but always having to sneak away with its tail between its legs.

Later, when I was older and hardened, I entertained my-self by observing his carefully calculated friendliness in his relationships with other people, and I was tempted to show him the arithmetic: a respectful bow and two squeezes of the hand for a man of high degree, an elegant bow to a woman of high degree, a smile and a nod to the most important clerks, a quick nod to the oldest hired men, and then his friendliness was used up. He had no more to expend.

As for the eight daughters in our flock, he said "sweet-heart" to us all, but he never called us by name. I, who knew that I was his love child and who thought I ought to have been the apple of his eye, never received a glance. Not even at parting.

The words bored themselves into Tora's memory and sent waves of recognition through her. Horrified, she read again and again:

> *. . . and I was ashamed of being unimportant, a nonen-tity in his life. How I made myself miserable with worry over what I had done wrong! How I strove to attain his praise!*

It was possible to read here what Tora had never con-fided to anyone, not even herself. She felt exposed and she became furious. It took time until she was able to perceive that it was not *her* futile love and sorrow Sunniva had written about. But by then the harm had already been done. The scab had been ripped from the sore, which would bleed freely for a long time to come.

"Is there anything I can do for you?"

The voice was earnest and warm.

Slowly she turned back to the light in the room.

"You are suffering, child. Will you talk to me about it?"

It was an odd question. Strange, unusual.

The Benefactor sat quite still and waited. He tried not to stare at her. But she felt that his glance was just as sympathetic as his voice.

She looked away, frightened that her eyes were so naked that he would see and understand everything. Maybe he would laugh at her childish desperation.

"You've never asked for anything since you came here to the hospital, Tora. But you have given a great deal to others. Don't you think I know that? Don't look away, child! Look at me while I add up all your fine deeds!"

He laughed, and his laughter was reflected in his eyes as he talked. Suddenly she herself had to laugh, flustered by his good-natured and personal interest.

"It's good to see that you can still laugh," he said, relieved.

Suddenly he grasped her hands. "I wanted to say this to you, because it's time for you to accept help. You must allow others to do for you as you have done for them. Now that you yourself are so ill, you must permit them to show their gratitude."

Why indeed should anyone bother about how she was doing? About whether she was living or dead?

"I can read your face like an open book, Tora," he said seriously. "You shouldn't think so poorly of your neighbors. It's arrogant to believe that no one can give you anything. You have no reason to despise yourself. You know better than that, don't you?"

She blushed. "I need nothing!"

She carefully tried to free her hands from his firm grasp.

"It's surely difficult to admit, but you need the love of both human beings and God. You, like all the others."

He did not loosen his hold on her hands.

She bowed her head so he wouldn't see her tears.

"You cannot relive her life," he said calmly. "She lived her life as best she could. She bore her shame with her head high. Believe me, God has forgiven all her sins and looked upon her poor soul with mercy. Let the dead bury the dead, Tora!"

She sobbed.

But no matter how deeply she buried her sorrow, it was of course alive anyway!

He stroked her cheek gently. "It is your eternal life that matters now, child, and your last days on earth." It sounded like a warning, and at once she grew dizzy.

"When you are ready to talk, I will be pleased to listen," he said quietly.

She wanted to, but she lacked the words to describe her desperation. Maybe she would not find the words in time.

"I have also come on a sad errand, Tora. We must amputate your feet, and it must be done tomorrow." He drew a deep breath, but he continued immediately without looking at her. "You've surely felt that it would have to happen, for you know, of course, that it's the only way to stop the decay. Fortunately, as busy as he is, the surgeon will be able to come. So we are spared from fetching just any old mustache trimmer. The surgeon is very talented in the art of healing, and he works quickly. It will be over faster than you can imagine, and I'll be there the whole time."

He smiled and gave her hands a little squeeze before he left.

The sunbeams that slanted through the window's uneven glass had an odd color pattern, which she hadn't noticed before. She watched as the slender flames of light changed from green to red to blue and thought how foolish she had been. She had lost herself in sorrow over a hopeless love and had not even let herself be bothered by the stench of death from her feet. Not until now did she understand that she could never again walk nor ever escape.

19

hey laid her on the table, stretched out and bound, with her feet over the edge so that the blood could run down into the bucket below. It was for her own good, they said, so she wouldn't suddenly jerk as the surgeon sawed and cut.

She could think of nothing but an animal prepared for slaughter.

Her hands were ice-cold and numb, as if she had long held them in cold water. She had to flex her fingers the whole time to be certain that they were still alive. Her eyes were glued to the ceiling as she listened to the clear, hard sounds of the instruments that the surgeon was placing on the table, one by one.

She tried to recognize the instruments by the sounds she remembered from all the times she herself had been present and held the hands of those who had to go through this operation. The big saw and the little one, the chisel and the sharp knife, the hammer and the little axe. All had different sounds, like warning bells with different clangings.

She couldn't remember in which order the instruments were used, for when she had been present to hold other patients, she had been busy just trying not to vomit. Now she suddenly wished that she knew whether he was going to use the knife or the saw first.

No matter which, it would be more horrible than she could imagine.

As soon as the Benefactor had told her about the operation, Tora had regretted her thoughtlessness. She had long since stopped examining her body each morning, even though that was *her* way of controlling the leprosy. *Her* secret exorcism. She who had nearly convinced herself that leprosy could be held captive, like a wild animal in a cage, if she were patient and meticulous in following the rules. But when the leprosy continued to grow and spread in spite of her daily examinations, she grew discouraged. It seemed futile to believe that she could be luckier than all the others around her. She knew only too well that everyone at the hospital had dreamed of escaping with the help of secret exorcisms or prayers, pacts with the netherworld or with God.

This was the punishment for her having treated her body like a despised shell, for her having stopped listening for, and paying attention to, its changes. Now she was going to lose her feet, without even knowing if there still was life beneath their hornlike crusts. Fragile life that the surgeon could not possibly see. Life that only she would have known about. If she had listened carefully.

At the moment the surgeon tightened his grip hard around her left shin she felt her foot quiver with life. And as the knife cut its way into her ankle bone, she could see before her that narrow, smooth foot running through the grass.

She bit into the stick between her teeth so hard that her jaws were locked in cramps. The howl of pain came from somewhere far back in her throat and drowned out the sound of bone being scraped and chiseled clean. Her heart hammered against her ribs, and she felt her breath, with dizzying speed, drawing her throat together against a spiral of light and blood-red darkness.

"Quick! Take the stick out before she is choked by foam!"

The air was light and bubbling, and the spiral turned slowly around on itself.

The Benefactor held her head between his hands. She stared up into his eyes, and as trusting as a little child she let herself be rocked until she was calm in his warmth.

"Your Father is with you," he whispered, and held her close with his glance, while the surgeon removed the other foot at the ankle, while the edges of the wound were singed, the blood stanched, and the bandages put on. The whole time he talked to her as if she were his most precious child.

The first days after the operation she was all alone in the bedroom and could cry without being ashamed, while Marthe placed leeches on the wounds. Maybe Marthe had placed the gruff old woman and the little girls in other rooms. Maybe they were all dead. She didn't ask for an explanation. She could think only about no longer having her feet. The pain after the operation was not as bad as her sorrow over their loss and her feeling of being to blame for it herself.

If only she had continued to tend herself with salves and medicines just as carefully as she had earlier tended the other patients!

It was too late now. She just had to accustom herself to her feet being gone and concentrate on keeping her balance on her knees. For she couldn't bear crawling like a snail for the rest of her life, as so many of the others did.

The operation had been a warning. That, she was more and more convinced of. Perhaps a sign. From whom she didn't know, but there were moments when she nearly felt a sort of gratitude. The strong feeling that someone had held a hand over her, someone had warned her, made her firmly determined not to die in the most pitiful way, bit by bit. And she wouldn't lose her hands. She had to keep them at any price. Her hands that could write her thoughts on white sheets of paper that others could read and that would ensure her a life after death.

She began to study her hands carefully.

Ever since she had come to the hospital her hands had been swollen and hurting badly. They quickly became feverishly warm or icy cold. Her palms were often sore and full of cracks. Between her fingers there were open sores, and on the backs of her hands and her fingers boils grew as hard as nails. But for one reason or another she did not lose the feeling in her hands or, much worse, lose her fingers, as she had seen so many others do.

How could that be? Was it really God's work?

Or had she helped herself without being aware of it?

She thought about the work she had had in the hospital, and she remembered her hands washing with water sudsy from strong green potash soap; her hands mixing tar salves; her hands bathed in turpentine and in decoctions of hop flowers; her hands crushing elm leaves and bark, stirring the juice of scabious and borax; her hands dripping with stinging vinegar. Those ailing hands that were always working with the medicines that helped against leprosy.

Slowly she grew certain about what she should do.

On the fourth day after the operation, she asked Marthe for help in getting out of bed and over to her chair in the hall.

"It's good that you asked." Marthe smiled. "I actually

came to suggest it myself. You've lain around lazily long enough! Now you must get up and walk."

"Don't joke!"

"I'm not joking, little sparrow. Just wait, you'll see."

Marthe briskly lifted her and carried her out into the hall.

The men and the women were sitting at the table as usual. They were cutting and braiding and knitting as usual, but their eyes clung to her as Marthe walked toward the tall windows. Around her chair the flock of children were waiting. On the center of the seat lay a beautiful wreath of fragrant meadow flowers. Leaning against the chair was a pair of crutches, new and immaculate, like freshly scrubbed wood.

"Kristoffer Wheelwright has made the crutches especially for you. They ought to fit just right," said Marthe, and gave a little toss of her head toward the blind old man at the table. "Remember to thank him really loudly!" she quickly whispered.

"What do you think I am? Don't you think I have any manners?" hissed Tora. "Help me up on them, then I'll show you!"

"As you like!"

Marthe smiled and called over her shoulder, "Olaf, come here! Here's a girl who won't wait!"

The ungainly boy with the freckled face came closer, and Tora suddenly remembered his mother and her howls of pain during the last part of her life, remembered all the nights she herself had made soothing drinks for her. Remembered the desperate eyes in that tired boyish face and his grateful look when Tora managed to convince his mother to drink and her howls quieted down.

"But you're well, aren't you? What are you still doing here?" she said, surprised.

He blushed terribly. "I'm doing the Lord's will," he said solemnly. "Mother and I were living in the most wretched need before we came to the hospital. Before we came, she was cast out and scorned by everyone, but here she met with mercy among people and found salvation in the Lord."

"Olaf is living in the Healthy Room together with the healthy poor. He is exceptionally helpful," said Marthe. "And he'll teach you to use the crutches."

There was nothing Tora would rather have. She needed help.

Olaf was also exceptionally patient. Never did his expression show that he thought she was childish and stupid when she raged about the crutches, which refused to obey her. When she cried with pain and desperation, he just calmly lifted her up from the floor and gently placed her on her chair. While she sat there and fought against the desire to give up, he began to fix the crutches.

"I'll just whittle here and there, then we can continue," he said consolingly.

As she stomped around in the hall, he followed. Each day that passed, she felt that the crutches were safer and she became better at using them. Soon it no longer bothered her that everyone kept close watch and gave her good advice.

The sisters Agnes and Kristin were always there. Like two little shadows they followed every shaky step she took. They never smiled and never talked. Just followed along and waited.

The day that she managed to go all alone from the bedroom to the chair by the window, they quietly disappeared outside. Soon after, they came in again with a large bouquet of flowers.

"It's for you," said Agnes, and curtsied to her.

"Will you read to us now?" said Kristin, and curtsied just as deeply.

"What do you want to hear?"

"Something so remarkable that no one has ever experienced anything like it," called blind Kristoffer.

She made herself comfortable and opened *Gulliver's Travels*. That had to be a book that was amazing enough. She already looked forward to the travels and to feeling a warmth against her knees.

he Benefactor came every day, but he seldom had time to stop and visit with anyone. He was clearly worn and worried.

"It's the same everlasting problem that's bothering him," said Marthe with a sigh when Tora asked. "Money. The hospital always has too little money for the support and care of the patients. We have managed tolerably well now for a couple of months. Alms have come often enough for all of you to receive the most necessary food and medicines. But autumn will soon be here, and I know the Benefactor fears another severe winter with great scarcity of food and unemployment in the town. That will make hate and fear flame up again and will strike the hospital with hunger and death. I know that he is doing his utmost so that the high authorities will give the hospital enough from the state treasury to do some good."

"Isn't there something we ourselves can do?" asked Tora.

"Not much, I'm afraid. It was different in the past; then the ailing had permission to sell what they made. But now that there is a lack of work for everyone, the cobblers and woodworkers' guild has denied the sick the right to sell clogs, ladles, and brooms. It's hard, for many here are capable craftsmen, and other than their work, the poor people have nothing to sell."

"I know of something that can be sold," said Tora suddenly. "Something that someone will pay dearly for. I have thought about it for quite some time."

Then she told Marthe the whole story of Sunniva and her powerful father.

Marthe turned flushed and pale, each after the other. "It's downright shameful!"

Tora understood that she was also thinking of her own treatment of Sunniva.

But she would not take part in Tora's plan. "It's impossible," she merely said. "The Benefactor will never go along with it. He is integrity itself."

"It's no crime to offer Sunniva's father the chance to buy her possessions," protested Tora vehemently. "After all, if he won't buy them, we can sell them at the market. We'll certainly get a good price there. I know that Sunniva wouldn't have anything against her possessions being of help to the ailing."

"And what did you want to use the money for?" Marthe couldn't keep from asking.

"Enough medications for the whole winter. Do you remember what you told me? That earlier, when times were good, you could get cartloads of vinegar, borax salt, mustard seed, turpentine, wax, and honey from the Swan Apothecary?"

Marthe nodded. "What a blessing to know that we had enough when winter came!"

"It can be like that again," said Tora, determined. "And I can help you to make salves and decoctions and everything else we need. But first we must follow my plan. The Benefactor need never learn where the money came from."

That didn't ease Marthe's mind any. For her, not telling was the same as lying. But with Tora's assurance that she could get the help she needed from Olaf, Marthe smiled with relief.

"Then I don't need to know more. You won't get my blessing, but I fervently hope that we can be spared another winter of death!"

Tora prepared to write the very first letter of her life. She knew that it would be difficult, for it was the most important letter she would ever write. She sat awake a whole night with Sunniva's diary open in her lap, inkwell and pen at the ready.

The blank sheets of paper stared up at her without giving any answer as to how she should express herself. It was important to be extremely careful, for she had to avoid his being offended or angry. Then he might complain to the Benefactor, and it would be impossible to carry out her plan. But neither must she express herself so carefully that he simply ignored the letter.

Tora pondered and wrote and rejected.

She read Sunniva's whole diary several times, and each time she felt the same pain as she read:

> Since I had left Bergen, it had grown larger beneath my heart. I had suspected it, and perhaps he had had the same fearful suspicion. What I didn't realize was the scope of his power. It was quickly made clear to me in the cloister that I carried death beneath my heart. In the cloister of the Holy Virgin there was no room for a fatherless child. But they said something else. They explained that I had all the signs of having a stillborn child, and when the time came, I was nearly convinced of it myself and therefore grateful that the priest was present and could place the child right in the lap of Our Lord. I was so trusting that I believed the nuns when they denied that she screamed at the moment she came into the world. But her scream continued to ring in my ears, and I understood that she was protesting against being robbed of the right to life.

How great was his fault for this?

Tora didn't know, but she suspected that his fault was great enough. For he had arranged for Sunniva to be brought back to Norway when he learned that she was sick and that her mother was dead of leprosy.

Perhaps there had been embraces that could not stand the light of day. Perhaps that was the reason for his having sent her away. It didn't matter. Sunniva's life was over. It wouldn't hurt him to pay a small indulgence.

Eventually she was satisfied with the letter.

It was polite and respectful, and she made it perfectly clear that her errand was to give Sunniva a good posthumous reputation. It would be remembered as a nobel deed if Sunniva contributed, after her death, to keeping other sufferers alive. That was the purpose of Tora's humble prayer for a donation of money to the hospital, in exchange for the chest labeled with Sunniva's real name and filled with all her personal possessions. Tora worked hard to explain why she was keeping the books. So it was in a natural way that she managed to mention that Sunniva's diary was in her hands and that she would destroy it before she herself died.

Olaf took the letter down to the shipyard offices on the wharf and waited until he could hand it to that powerful man in person. Sunniva's father had opened it then and there, Olaf related when he came back, while he himself watched. The great man had turned as pale as a ghost, but he had said only that Tora would have to wait for a message.

Tora waited tensely.

One day passed after the other without anything happening, and doubt began to gnaw at her. Had she miscalculated? Was he less proud than she had counted on? Or did he just want to keep her on tenterhooks for a time? Perhaps he was planning a terrible revenge.

No matter what happened, it was too late to turn back.

She began to prepare to sell the chest at the market and pondered for a long time over how she should arrange it. She dreaded her plan now. It suddenly seemed dangerous, almost as if a trap had been set for her.

Then one day there was a thunderous knock at the gate.

Right afterward Marthe came breathlessly into the hall. "The great gentleman has sent people here to get the chest!"

"Thank goodness! It's packed and ready!"

Tora was so relieved that she shook.

Some days later, the Benefactor came over and sat down directly opposite her, just as he had done once before.

Tora, who had been yearning to talk to him for such a long time, suddenly grew uneasy. She couldn't bear to see the disappointment in his eyes or to hear him say that what she had done was sinful. She began to talk about her feet and the crutches and anything else she could hastily think of, anything that could prevent his asking her about the letter and the chest.

Marthe had told her that the Benefactor had wondered a great deal about the large anonymous donation of money that had recently come to the hospital. It wasn't unusual that donors refrained from stating their names, but this nameless donor was unusually generous and obviously knew that the hospital needed medicine.

Marthe had fled into the hall to escape having to be dishonest.

Now, perhaps, it was Tora's turn.

"I have something to tell you," said he, and looked right into her eyes.

Here it comes, she thought. Never in the world would she dare to look him in the eyes as she confessed.

"But, child, why won't you look at me?" he said almost sadly. "Is there something wrong?"

She didn't answer.

"If you think I have been with you too little recently, you must realize that I have no choice. Great things, you know, have been happening. Our country now has its own government. The new parliament must not tolerate the hospital's being a cemetery for the living. Its shameful privation must cease, and I must use all my strength to fight for the patients' cause. I'm unable to do anything else."

Tora grew dizzy with relief. He knew nothing. He had not come to scold her.

She leaned forward in her chair and laid her hand gently on his black sleeve. "But I've heard that alms have come from sympathetic citizens."

"Yes, and God be praised for that. Without the alms the distress would have been unbearable. Thanks to good sailors and citizens, many have escaped death from starvation."

He sighed.

"But we can't count on alms, and the sums are never large enough so that the wretched conditions at the hospital can be corrected. You know, of course, that the roofs are rotten and the buildings drafty. There are too many patients here in too small a space, and therefore the air is unhealthy and causes far too many to die of lung disease when the cold sets in. There is too little nutritious food, and never enough medicine. But the worst thing is that the hospital lacks a proper doctor."

"But you give us the best care and nursing we can get," she objected.

"Well, thank you!" He smiled sadly. "According to the best of my knowledge and ability. But I am not a doctor by profession. I can alleviate pain somewhat, but I don't know the art of healing well enough to prevent the greatest suffering that leprosy brings."

He grew quiet.

Tora waited attentively for him to continue.

It was as if he was confiding in her. She felt privileged.

"You are young and brave, Tora. You're quick to learn and you are persevering. You could have had a long and rich earthly life. But leprosy has robbed you of that possibility. It's all the more unreasonable that leprosy is so feared and loathed and so little is done to heal the illness. It's outrageous that many good Christians maintain that leprosy is God's punishment and that you are sinners being punished as you deserve."

"But the Bible says that . . ." began Tora.

He interrupted her vehemently: "Read the Bible carefully, Tora. Trust the Bible's word, not people's interpretation of it. But, of course, you haven't read the Bible yet?"

"No, not the whole of it."

She gave a sidelong glance up at him.

His face showed neither disappointment nor censure. He was completely immersed in his despair.

"There is so terribly much I would like to have done for all of you. But I don't have the strength to encompass it all."

He bowed his head.

Tora wished that she could say something consoling. But there was nothing to say.

"You have enough of your own sorrows, child, without having to bear mine as well."

"There is something I don't understand," she said softly.

"Just ask. I can explain problems more easily than I can solve them."

She wanted to say that he mustn't blame himself. That nothing would become better through his having a bad conscience. But she was afraid that he would think she was too bold.

"Why must we suffer because of the great war?"

He smiled sadly. "Indeed, that, my child, isn't easy to understand. Neither is it fair. Unfortunately, the effects of a war are like rings in water. Even the smallest stone that's thrown makes large rings. One can never be certain what is really being struck. War is, in itself, a terrible waste of life. Moreover, the innocent far from the battlefields are always stricken with hunger, suffering, and poverty."

The Benefactor explained how the wars of the Emperor Napoleon of France led to war between the dual kingdom of Norway-Denmark and England, which in turn led to Norway's not being able to import grain or to export its fish. When stores ran out, the price of grain rose enormously in Norway. But without trade with other countries, the value of money in Norway decreased. In the wake of that devaluation, there followed unemployment and privation.

"You can imagine for yourself the ring effects in Bergen, the busiest market town in the country. The situation has lasted very long now, seven whole years, and yet it doesn't look as if it's improving. This year I'm afraid we'll have an extremely dangerous summer in town, for there is great unrest among the peasants. Do you understand better now?"

"I understand the connection," said Tora aloud.

But she didn't say that it was incomprehensible to her that God let people do such terrible things to one another without stepping in. She knew that the Benefactor had an explanation, but she couldn't bear to hear it now.

"I hope you understand that it isn't from maliciousness that people stop giving alms," he said. "Neither can anyone be blamed because the hospital, which earlier had a good income from its lands, is now itself a poorhouse. And when catastrophes strike, they always affect the defenseless the most. It seems to be the rule for catastrophes," he finished bitterly.

He sounded more hopeless than ever.

All at once Tora was extremely glad that she had forced Sunniva's father to pay so royally for the chest, for they were assured medicine for a long time to come.

Each of them got a splash of milk every day, now that the hospital's three milk cows were out on lush pasture all day long. It was going worse with the rye and potatoes.

But Tora had been hungry many times before, when the crops had failed on the mountain farms. That gnawing hunger was not what she feared the most. The worst thing was the thought of the bitingly cold and wet winter that was coming. A winter when she could expect to be a victim of lung disease.

"If only this summer would last a really long time!"

"Let's sincerely hope it does." The Benefactor smiled and got up. "You know what? It helped to get that off my chest."

He stroked her hair. "Actually, I was going to tell you something far more gratifying. Your father visited me today. He didn't know that you were still alive. He wants to see you."

"No!"

"But, child, what are you thinking? Won't you see your own father?"

No! she thought. That's not how it is at all! After all, it

was he who wouldn't see her. It was he who knew that the parish pastor had waited for him to say goodbye to her, and it was he who remained sitting by the rapids as the pastor's cart drove off. She could still hear that wailing melody.

But she could never explain any of that to the Benefactor.

"Things aren't well with your father. I understand that he is burdened by a great sorrow. Make him welcome, Tora," said the Benefactor sternly. "I ask you to remember that forgiveness is the greatest of all virtues."

After he left, she remained sitting as if paralyzed. What should she do? Could she prevent his coming? She didn't want to feel hope, longing, and defeat anew.

For the rest of her life, she wanted only to be at peace with herself in the world of books.

She shut her eyes to stop the dizziness.

Her bad dream was really here.

21

ora opened her eyes wide.

Panic shook her wide-awake.

She couldn't breathe!

She swallowed and swallowed, but her throat was closed. Her breath could get neither in nor out. She sat up and gasped desperately. A violent coughing fit finally loosened the phlegm that closed her windpipe. She stared as it ran down on the blanket. No, it was clear and shiny. Without a trace of blood.

Relieved, she sank back on the pillow and drew her breath in careful drafts. She was thoroughly soaked with perspiration, which ran in small streams from her forehead and mixed in with her tears.

A warning this time.

It was the air in the bedroom that had given her a feeling of choking. It was dense with illness and warmth. And the summer was drier and hotter than any summer she could remember. Days and nights passed without one hearing the wind whistling through the steep, narrow passageways or the hulls grumbling against one another in the wind-tossed waves in Vågen, Bergen's harbor. Without hearing the sheets on the clotheslines behind the hospital flapping like billowing sails in the wind.

If only the window could stay open at night! Then it wouldn't be so intolerable to awaken to a new suffocating day. But the snappish old woman from Arna wouldn't allow it. And Tora didn't protest, for she knew what an uproar would result from crossing "the Arna Raven."

It was blind Kristoffer who had started calling her that. Not aloud. That, he didn't dare. Not any longer.

She was like a raven. A heavy and ill-omened bird.

At first they had only noticed that she whined more than most. But she was extremely ill with fever when she came and they had thought that it would probably soon be over. Tora, who had to share a bedroom with her, was expecting it. But as if through a miracle, the old woman revived.

From that moment they knew that she would watch them and everything they did and never let a chance pass to complain and scold and mumble threateningly about God's righteous judgment over sinful people.

Sadly, they had been proved right.

With the Arna Raven the hospital was transformed into a virtual mausoleum. It was as if she shoveled black sod over laughter and play, which were to be found here in spite of everything. Their joy, which could unexpectedly blaze up, they did everything to safeguard. Suddenly it had become sinful to play in the house of death, and with sin came self-righteousness and tattling.

Marthe had had great difficulty convincing the Arna Raven to let Tora lie in the bedroom alone for a few days after her operation. Every day she took up a position in the doorway to glare accusingly from Tora to the empty bed. Tora had heard Marthe ask her to be patient, but she only answered firmly that she had to live in that room. Because it lay nearest the outer door, she said. She repeated it so often and so loudly that they all had the same feeling of being in peril.

Something awful could happen at any time. Like a fire, for example. There were often fires in the town of Bergen, and once, the hospital had burned completely to the ground. That was a hundred years ago, but no one knew when it might happen again. They had to be on their guard. They had to be prepared for the worst. God was their only protector.

The Arna Raven got her way and soon moved back into the bedroom. She had collected a loyal crowd of listeners for her fulminations about the ungodliness that ruled in the hospital. The church soon resounded day and night with loud prayers and dirges, sobs and acts of penance. The Arna Raven was enthroned uppermost by the altar and kept sharp watch that their fervor was satisfactory.

It was like an epidemic, thought Tora darkly. A contagious possession by fear. It was eerie. She was simply waiting for the old woman to turn against her with accusations of sacrilege or something worse. Tora tried to make herself invisible on her chair with her books. But she no longer dared to read aloud, for she knew that the Arna Raven believed that there was only one true book to be found in the world. All others were sinful.

The Arna Raven completely and entirely filled one of the beds in the little room. Tora was happy she had been able to keep the mattress on the floor between the beds. It was bad enough to have to tolerate that endless stream of predictions about the end of the world without also having to be squeezed flat each night by that heavy body.

The Arna Raven was self-righteous and heartless, and Tora wholeheartedly disliked her. It was like hearing and seeing her own grandmother. The same tight mouth, the same glance, and the same tone when she thundered, "Remember that this is death's house!" at every little thing she didn't like.

As if everyone didn't know that!

As if they did anything besides think about their own death.

As if everyone didn't fear God's wrath on that last day.

That was exactly why they were so vulnerable.

Tora knew that for Kristin, the older of the little girls, the Arna Raven's fire-and-brimstone sermons were pure torture. She cried herself to sleep every single night. Not even her little sister's whispered solace could soothe her fear.

Now they were asleep with their arms protectively around each other. As long as they slept, they could at least be in peace from the threats of eternal torture in hell. Worriedly, Tora saw that they had become extremely thin of late. They were more like two ruffled baby birds than angels of God's mercy.

The hospital was a true hell this summer.

Whether it was the heat or the food that was the cause, she didn't know. Marthe maintained that it was owing to the two barrels of salted herring they had received from an unknown donor sometime in early summer. The fish was spoiled, she said. That was the cause of the cramps, vomiting, diarrhea, and death that struck everyone, the leprous as well as the healthy.

The two little girls were also stricken. Tora felt more compassion for them than for most of the others, for they were inseparable. She hoped that they would be able to die together, but she feared that Kristin's time would come first. She seemed sicker and weaker than little Agnes. She was also more afraid, and fear could push one more quickly toward death, Tora knew.

Tora assured herself that the others were sleeping before she began her daily investigation of her body. She started as usual with her legs. The wounds from the operation were completely healed now. Her ankle bones had become round marbles covered by shiny red flesh. They still hurt to step on when she used the crutches, but it was nothing in comparison to the pain in the beginning. The inflammation was entirely gone, and no new boils had yet appeared on her legs. She could tell that the clusters of boils around her nose, along her cheekbones, and down toward her throat had become larger. This meant that she had to bathe them more often in the decoction of hop flowers. Otherwise the sickness would soon eat its way into the bone.

Her right hand was unchanged, and she still had full use of her aching fingers. It was worse with the left. That arm was paralyzed from her elbow to her fingers.

Her fingers looked terrible, and she knew that she would soon awaken one morning to find that they had fallen off her hand. The fingers would lie beside her like little dead animals. She would cry over them for a long time. Because they were gone. Because death was drawing so much closer, and she would soon have to make a decision.

But, before that, she would bury the fingers in the hospital yard, under the little wooden cross where she had put Sunniva's finger to rest so long ago, just after she herself had come to the hospital.

There was a tiny birch tree growing on the grave. Tora didn't know how the tree had ended up there. She hadn't planted it. But there it stood, now two years old. Each spring it grew a little taller, stronger, and lusher. Nowhere else in the yard were birch trees growing.

Perhaps human beings became trees after they died. It

was a beautiful thought that nothing actually died but formed new life. That human beings lived on in another form.

> *Earth to earth,*
> *ashes to ashes,*
> *dust to dust.*

She hoped that someone would read that by her grave.

Perhaps in time she would be a magnificent birch that the winds could play in and birds build nests in. Then she could stand there thinking great thoughts about the world, just as the tree people did in Niels Klim's world beneath the earth.

Tora crept on her knees quickly toward the door where her crutches stood. She had to have some air. She wanted to go out into the yard to breathe in the last bit of the dewy fresh morning before it was devoured by the burning sun.

She knew it was wrong to hate the old woman. After all, she couldn't help it if she reminded Tora of all the times she had knelt before her Granny and repeated after her: *Thank you, sweet Jesus, for your punishment; redeem your sinful child from eternal damnation,* while blows rained down on her clasped hands.

Granny maintained that Tora's sins were as numerous as the stars in the sky. Therefore, she might just as well be punished every day.

Tora knew that most things were sins in Granny's eyes.

Therefore, she expected punishment every day. She tolerated the punishment, but she refused to accept that she deserved it.

That it was sinful to run into the church or to sit restlessly in the pew, she could understand. But to pick flowers for Jesus on the cross or to sing a little too loudly in His honor, she could never grasp as being a sin. It never helped to defend herself. Granny just chastised her even more severely.

Granny had kept a sharp watch on the whole family's sins, and she punished all of them equally hard with blows, words, or glances. No one dared to rebel against her or doubt that she alone had interpreted the Lord's will correctly. Not even Tora's father, though he was the head of the family.

Her father least of all, thought Tora bitterly.

Either he locked himself in the shed he used when making his fiddles or he knocked about from farm to farm or played the fiddle with the sprite of the waterfall. Then no one dared to disturb him. That's how he had avoided being present when Granny and Tora's mother had their clashes over her. That's how he escaped having to decide whether her grandmother was right that Tora had to be chastised into a fear of God or her mother was right that punishment was driving Tora away from God. All the same, her mother had always defended her father. But, of course, she had his love.

Tora's father, who had waited so long to find out if she

was alive. Who had said to the Benefactor that he wanted to see her. But who didn't come. Who made promises and never kept them.

She had used all her strength to repress old bitterness and to prepare herself for a reconciliation. But days had passed. The waiting was nearly unbearable. Her disappointment and shame grew greater and more painful. Then she began to doubt that she had heard right. Maybe she had been dreaming. A worse dream than that which tortured her each night.

She hadn't dared to ask the Benefactor if he was quite certain that her father had asked to see her. The Benefactor was more exhausted and overwhelmed than ever, and he seldom had time to do more than look in on the very sickest, hold church services, and conduct the all-too-frequent burials.

Tora had reached the outside door.

When she stood on her knees, she could just reach the door handle. First she opened the door. Then she began to pull herself up on the crutches. It took time. One slipped, and then the other. She had to have control over both when she hoisted herself up. Eventually she managed it. She was standing steady on the crutches, and they were securely under her arms. She stepped out on the crutches and turned her face toward the blindingly white sunlight.

The air was still crisp and morning fresh, and she drew it in, in full drafts.

"Is it you? Oh my God, is it really you . . ."

The voice was low, raw, and unrecognizable. It took a little time before she knew where it had come from.

She squinted in the sharp sunlight, over toward the green darkness by the gate.

"Who is it?"

She had to shade her eyes.

No one answered. But someone was breathing in quick gasps over there.

"Is that you, Endre?"

She still heard only that spasmodic breathing.

She knew, of course, that it wasn't Endre. For over a year no one had heard news of the vessel he had sailed on. Marthe had prepared her for the possibility of its never returning from its hunting trip to the ice west of Spitsbergen. Tora had not cried, for she knew that he was to be found somewhere or other and that a part of her was there, too.

Endre would never think of frightening her in this way.

"Come out now!" she said loudly and apprehensively.

Then suddenly she turned cold.

Maybe it was a robber or one of those furious peasants who had forced his way in. Marthe had said that there was more disturbance than usual in the town this summer. It was such that one could be downright fearful for one's life, said Marthe when she came back from the wharves or the street sellers' stalls.

Tora shuddered with a sense of approaching misfortune.

She wanted to reach safety behind the hospital door, and quickly. But she turned around too sharply and lost control of the crutches. Without being able to catch herself, she fell to the ground headfirst.

She heard herself cry in pain before she fainted.

Slowly she returned to pure pain stabbing through her head. She was not lying hard and miserable on the burning hot ground. She was lying softly in the lap of a man who was drying blood from her hair and dripping salt tears on her face.

"It's me, your father," said a voice that she had to strain to hear.

"It's me, Tora," he repeated, as if he knew that she didn't believe it.

She wanted to get away from what could not be true.

He didn't try to hold on to her.

She scrabbled up the steps.

"Don't look at me!" she snarled, and sniffled loudly.

He didn't move. Just sat in the white heat and didn't look at all like the cheerful father she had been expecting. The fiddle was the same, all right, but the bloated face, the graying hair, and the bent back she had never seen before. Nor had she seen the tattered clothing and the black desperation in his eyes.

t's a true blessing that you found your way here, Fiddler Mons. No one in this house of sorrow has heard a joyful melody in time out of mind! Surely you still play like the water sprite himself?"

Later blind Kristoffer maintained that he had recognized Tora's father the moment he came in with her in his arms. "You must never believe that the blind can't see!" he had jestingly said, as if offended with Tora. "One can see both a gait and a voice without eyes."

Tora thought that, rather, it was the ring of her father's fiddle that Kristoffer had recognized. She herself just wished that it wasn't her father.

He placed her on the chair with the high back. There she sat, refusing to look at him.

He plucked irresolutely at the fiddle strings with his bow.

But she was relieved when Kristoffer said, "Give us

a melody, Fiddler Mons. Then the day will start off right."

Her father did not need to be asked twice. He placed the fiddle under his chin and played a soft and lilting tune. The hall was filled with a playful summer wind and the stunning scent of flowers, and the sound enticed even the sickest away from their daily pains, bad dreams, and penance. Tora was delighted. Suddenly she caught a glimpse of adult merriment that she had never before seen in the hospital, a sensual joy in life that she herself would not get to experience.

When he finished, it was as if the light had gone out.

Tora knew that she was not alone in feeling the cold that rushed through the hall.

Her father noticed it also and put his bow to the strings again.

"Aren't you ashamed, you godless fiddler! How dare you dishonor the Lord in the house of death!"

The Arna Raven, wrapped in her great black shawl, stood in the hall.

Slowly she lifted her arms toward the sky and shouted: "God's punishment will strike us all! Our suffering now is nothing compared to the terrible, eternal tortures that await! His righteous wrath knows no bounds!"

She might just as well have whipped them, thought Tora angrily.

Old as well as young, men as well as women—all shrank back like naughty children beneath that terrific fire-and-brimstone sermon. As the Arna Raven pronounced judgments, each one more ghastly than the other, the hall was filled with desperate prayers for absolution.

The Arna Raven is worse than Granny, thought Tora! Tears stung her eyes.

This woman took more delight in scolding the sinners. Her threats of eternal torture and damnation were more merciless. Was there no one who dared to reply?

"You are wrong, grandmother," said Kristoffer calmly. "It isn't true that every little joy is an abomination before God. Our Heavenly Father knows our suffering on earth. He grants the most wretched of His children a little joy."

"You shall not take the Lord's name in vain!" the Arna Raven thundered. "You know that fiddle playing is the devil's work! It leads straight to whoring and carousing!"

"And who are you to dare judge us all in His name? Who has given you the right?" answered Kristoffer sharply. "Don't you think that we know Our God, each in his own way? In God's name, play, Fiddler Mons. Let your music remind us of the life He gave us, as it was and still ought to be!"

"Don't you dare!" screamed the Arna Raven.

"Don't let yourself be cowed!" roared blind Kristoffer just as angrily. "Fiddler Mons, do you hear! Play for *our* sakes, for *God's* sake! Don't let yourself be cowed!"

Tora didn't expect her father to dare what he had never dared before. She saw him lift his fiddle hesitantly and then let it fall again. She knew how much he hated to choose sides, a choice that he had always retreated from.

227

She met his glance and wanted to say that it was she who would lose the most if he fled.

He slowly rose and laid the fiddle carefully down beside Kristoffer. Then he walked over to the old woman and spoke quietly: "I'm going to play. But first you should know, grandmother, that I have recently buried someone like you. A mother who never had a good word for anyone. Not for her son, his children, or their mother. Never a loving thought or a forgiving word. Only threats and punishment and prophecies of eternal pain."

He drew a deep breath.

Tora saw that his hands were shaking.

"For all too long, she behaved as she wanted, for I wasn't home with those who needed me. I didn't dare be. I wasn't worthy of their love. I understood too late that life is meaningless without love. Therefore, old woman, I know that we owe Our Maker some sign of our joy and gratefulness for His having given us the privilege of life."

He put his hands on the old woman's shoulders and looked into her eyes for a long time.

"Listen carefully and think it over. When my mother died, I felt neither sorrow nor loss. Just relief. For to me she had always been death itself. She left nothing behind. It was as if she had never lived. Remember that. You still have time to find love for the life God has given you. Do so; then you will not have lived in vain."

Tora had never heard her father talk like that.

All at once she knew that it was not a speech to the old

woman that she was hearing but a plea for forgiveness meant for her.

Indeed, he had been aware of her.

He had just never dared to show it.

The old woman's reaction came as a total surprise.

Tora had expected her to be furious, to shower Tora's father with even more biting accusations and threats, but she did not. She just stood for a moment immobile, as if nailed to the floor. She stared at Tora's father with an open mouth and an expression on her face as though he had struck her. Then she burst into violent sobs. And while they looked on, she shrank into a quite ordinary person who feared the loss of her precious life just as much as they did theirs.

hey heard the shout for help before the door burst open and Olaf stumbled in.

He looked terrible. His face was battered, and his hands dripped with blood. "Help me!" he groaned. "Can't you hear me? It's Marthe! She's bleeding and bleeding! I didn't have the strength to carry her farther than to the yard."

No one moved. They only stared. Stunned.

"Don't you understand? Marthe is dying!" he howled still louder.

Then panic broke out.

Above the noise of wailing and sobbing, Tora heard someone shrieking and understood that it was she herself. She had managed to drag herself up on her crutches and was on her way toward the door when she was knocked flat by people who were circling senselessly about.

"Didn't you hear me calling for help?" screamed Olaf.

"Haven't you heard the noise from the fight between the peasants and the town authorities?"

"The end of the world is near! Praise the Lord! All shall be judged in the last days!"

The Arna Raven was herself again. Her triumphant shout was like oil on fire. Stricken with terror, some began to fall to their knees, some tried to crawl to the church, but others fainted from fright.

Even above the terrible noise in the hall, they suddenly heard it, like waves breaking against a distant shore. The sounds of blows and shots, loudly shouted commands, and the roars of a raging mob.

"It's a hell out there!" cried Olaf. "There are bleeding people everywhere, and God only knows how many have been trampled underfoot!"

"Silence!" roared blind Kristoffer. He had climbed up on the bench. "Have you completely lost your minds? Marthe is lying out in the yard in need of help, and here you are running around like chickens with their heads cut off. Come to your senses!"

Tora had managed to free herself from those who had fallen over her and was scrabbling quickly toward the door. She wanted to get out to Marthe! Even if she had to knock someone unconscious to make her way.

Then she saw her father run out, with Olaf at his heels.

Soon after, he was back, with Marthe in his arms. He walked slowly toward the table and laid his lifeless burden gently down.

No one moved. Not a sound was to be heard as Tora hobbled over to the table.

Marthe must have been struck on the temple by a large stone. The wound was deep and had bled profusely. But now the blood was congealed and dark. In that colorless face only the lips shone, with a deathly blue color.

Tora put her mouth close to Marthe's ear. "You promised to be here always," she whispered. "Now you have gone ahead of me. I shall tend you myself. Maybe your gown won't be as fine as you deserve, but it will be as beautiful as I'm now able to sew it."

Tora's father and Olaf carried Marthe to her room behind the kitchen.

There was no one on duty there now. Marthe had been doing the work in the hospital alone for several weeks.

Tora sent a little lad off with a message for the Benefactor.

There was a lot to be done, and she didn't know where to begin. She herself could manage so little. All at once she felt herself to be endlessly tired and discouraged. Not only had Marthe left her; she had also taken with her all the order, common sense, and care that kept them together.

"We'll manage it some way, Tora. You and I." Blind Kristoffer sat down beside her.

"The blind leading the lame," she mumbled tiredly.

"That's not so bad when the blind can get people to obey and the lame are as smart as you." He smiled. "The Benefactor will probably be here soon and figure out what to do. In the meantime, get Olaf to tell us what actually happened. Otherwise people will go crazy with worry."

That morning at dawn Olaf had gone with Marthe down to the wharf. They wanted to see if they could find a fisherman who was willing to give an extra good measure for the few coins they had. When they were passing the town hall, they saw that people were starting to assemble there, and Marthe had immediately gathered that they were peasants from hamlets like Arna and Åsane. Peasants who had long protested against the high price of grain.

"They've come to force the merchants to lower the price," Marthe had said. "And they'll probably not give up before they get their way."

She had wanted to turn around, but Olaf refused to listen with more than half an ear. Neither of them thought that the dispute would develop so quickly and so violently.

When they came back with a batch of fresh fish, the battle was already in full swing. The furious peasants had stormed the town hall and brought out the merchants by force. They chased the merchants, like rats, from the attic of the town hall, where some of them had tried to hide. It was said that even the prefect, when he showed himself, was chased away with a stick.

Marthe was nervous and wanted to return to the hospital immediately, but Olaf had convinced her to wait a little while. If there was anything he fervently wished, it was for the peasants to get the better of those bloodsucking merchants. Because of them his own family had lost everything and he and his mother were forced to go begging in Bergen. He had only wanted to stand a moment and shake his fist along with the others, but suddenly it was too late to get away. When the soldiers stormed in, he suddenly found himself between them and the peasants, who only grew angrier that the authorities had set the soldiers on them. In the hailstorm of cudgel blows, Olaf was knocked out, and when he came to, he couldn't find Marthe. At first he thought that she had gotten away; then he discovered her. She lay at the edge of the battle, immobile and bleeding. He dragged her back to the hospital.

They listened with bowed heads.

The silence lasted long after Olaf had finished talking.

"See, I was right! Pity the one who doubts God's wrath!" The old woman rose and strode toward the church. A black avenging angel. "There is only one salvation. At the altar."

No one any longer had the strength or courage for doubt. They all followed the old woman to the church. Those who could walk by themselves, those who had to crawl, those who had to be carried by others.

Only Tora stayed in the hospital.

She wanted to search the night nurses' room for Marthe's very finest linen cloth. The cloth that she knew Marthe had hidden for her.

But first she had to find the little girls.

They were where they had hidden themselves when all the turmoil began, beneath the blanket on their bed. They had fallen asleep from terror and exhaustion.

For a long time she sat looking at the two of them, so tightly entwined that they were breathing each other's breath. For a moment she envied their inseparability. To think and feel as one person. But separation, she knew, would be all the more painful for them.

Tora listened anxiously to the distant sounds of the battle in front of the town hall.

Had he gone there? she wondered. He had said nothing to her before he took his fiddle and disappeared.

It would be like him to turn all his attention toward a conflict that didn't concern him when she needed him more than ever before. She wished that she could be furious. He deserved nothing more. But in spite of everything, he had come. And she had known the taste of his tears and heard his plea for forgiveness. She couldn't do anything but listen anxiously to the battle and hope that he wouldn't be hurt.

The battle continued the whole hot day.

In the church the prayer lasted until late in the evening.

Many prayed for their sons and husbands who were fighting against the greed and poverty that the great war had created. They all prayed fervently that fire and plundering would not follow the conflict and perhaps also strike the hospital.

It had grown late before the battle quieted in front of the town hall.

The silence was hot and oppressive.

In the hospital hall the ill sat gathered in the dark and listened anxiously.

Was the battle over for the time being? Was this just the lull before a new storm? Or was there worse coming? No one dared to sleep while such horrible uncertainty reigned.

Olaf, who had recovered completely from the fright and injuries he had received that morning, offered to find out what had happened.

No one tried to prevent his going to the town hall again.

They waited silently until he came back.

It was all over, he told them, and they drew a breath of relief.

But many were injured. Exactly how many, no one knew. It wasn't as serious as one might have feared, for the soldiers had not been willing to attack the peasants quite as forcefully as the authorities had given orders to. There were many peasant sons among the soldiers, and they wouldn't follow orders to be brutal to their own people.

"But they arrested many peasants," continued Olaf excitedly. "And there will be big fines and public whippings and perhaps something even worse!"

That made the patients' anxiety increase again. But Olaf

could not tell them what had happened to their husbands and sons.

"There was hardly anyone left there when I arrived, and only one man that I knew. He was playing when I came and will probably continue to play until the whippings are over," Olaf said, and looked at Tora.

elp her!" the little girl had screamed, and had shaken Tora awake. Tora had tried as best she could to pump life back into the girl's thin body. But it was useless. She saw that by the girl's unwavering stare and felt it by the coolness of her skin. It was inconceivable. She was just eight years old, but her heart would not beat and her breath would not come. Yet she was smiling as if death were a game.

"She has gone to God."

Tora didn't know what else she could say to console little Agnes.

"You're lying! She promised we would always be together! She would not have gone without me!" She sobbed with fear and rage.

Tora quickly pulled her close.

"Hush! Don't cry so loudly! We don't want the old woman to wake up, do we?"

Agnes shook her head and peeked fearfully over Tora's shoulder at the broad back. They both knew what would happen if she awakened.

"Perhaps Kristin is so far away in her dreams that she doesn't hear you calling," said Tora.

It was terrible to lie about death, but she was too exhausted to manage the struggle of making the little girl understand right now. The truth would have to wait until tomorrow.

"Come lie down with me," she whispered. "Then your sister can rest in peace."

"I want to be where she is," said Agnes decisively.

She lay down next to her sister, with her arms around her neck and her mouth close to Kristin's ear.

Tora slept and dreamed about a cobalt-blue sky filled with gold-clad angels who resembled Sunniva and Marthe.

Marthe shouldn't have been there.

She should have been here.

Then Agnes would have voluntarily let go of her dead sister. She would have stopped screaming and kicking and would have come to her senses again far sooner. If only Marthe had been here. She who lovingly and firmly would have loosened the girl's grasp, embraced her, and rocked her until she could no longer bring herself to cry out. And while Agnes slept, they would have clad the sister, laid her in the coffin, and buried her before her sister awakened. You can't wait with funerals in this oppressive heat, Marthe would have said.

Now nothing would be as it might have been.

Tora had never seen such sorrow as little Agnes's. For several days she lay lifelessly. She didn't even notice when they loosened her grasp and lifted up her sister.

Tora had really never felt the sorrow of another so severely.

Perhaps it was wrong not to let her be present at the funeral. Now she refused to believe that her sister was dead. But she no longer sobbed; she just lay curled up in the bed and waited. It was eerie to see that she was lying as if pressed close to her invisible sister.

Even though she lay quite still, it was as if a terrible storm were raging in the room.

Tora found no rest and no shelter. She could only lie awake night after night and feel that mute sorrow making her ever weaker.

The overwhelming tiredness frightened her, but simultaneously she felt strangely calm. The tiredness filled her body like water. It made it difficult to move and painful to breathe. She had to struggle to keep awake, but still she couldn't sleep. She couldn't think, and yet she had one clear thought in her mind:

Come now, death. Wait no longer.

25

he was surrounded by light, white-hot rays of light that, in steadily greater spirals, spun inward and outward across enormous night-blue space.

There was no end to be found, she knew. Or beginning.

Just endless, shining time that was older than space could remember.

Time was sound, a voice of pulsating time formed before the beginning of language.

The voice did not speak to her or to the light that rushed between mighty worlds of slowly rotating darkness.

That wordless voice was inside her and outside in the infinite,

deep and vibrating from a power like a huge beating heart without sorrow or pain or love,

but full of exultant delight over life's invincibility.

She listened and understood why she had received the gift of life.

This moment was life
now and in all eternity.

For a long time she heard but the one voice that embraced all time, all light, all space.

Then she heard a myriad of voices.

Humming, laughing, talking, they streamed toward her, through her.

We have been granted voices,
she heard them say, and she knew that they were Sunniva, her mother, and Marthe.

We have come to answer whatever you may ask.

Does God exist? Is there a heaven and a hell? she asked, and immediately regretted her childish questions.

Little sparrow, can you never learn to trust in your own knowledge?

That was Sunniva's laughter, she thought, ashamed.

Of course there exists a God and all other gods in their cobalt-blue or gilded heavens and heavens of stardust.

Hell exists in all the forms by which you can ever desire to torment yourself.

She was silent, but they heard her question anyway.

Gods and heavens and hells are to be found within you created by you when you ask about the meaning of life when you can't bear carrying the lonely responsibility a human being has for her life and for the survival of the world.

Is that all?
No—time our mother is everything,
time that no one can stop and no one can change.
Little sparrow
from time have you come
to time shall you return
from time shall you rise again and again

The doorway was suddenly filled with a darkness denser than darkness itself.

"I have come to take you home with me," said he.

"Do you have the fiddle with you?"

He smiled and nodded.

"Do you know where I want to go?" said she.

"There where we both want to go, I imagine. Where she is waiting for us."

She tried to rise without waking little Agnes, who was sleeping in her arms, but the child awoke at once, as if she had been waiting for this moment.

"You can't leave without me," she said. "No one shall leave me again."

Her thin face shone with obstinance.

"But you can't go along. Where we are going is all too far."

"I can fly," she answered just as firmly. "I have wings of light and fire. They will bear me everywhere as I search for her."

"But you are so young, little sparrow."

Tora felt herself helplessly trapped between right and wrong.

"It is her life, you know," he said quietly. "Young in years she may be, but old in sorrow and pain. Let her decide for herself. There will always be a way when the time comes."

There was little that Tora wanted to take along. She didn't need the crutches anymore, for he preferred to carry her on his back. She took only Sunniva's diary. She had promised it would disappear with her. Once, she had dreamed of writing in the book, so that a little part of herself would exist on paper that someone could then read. But there had never been time, and now it was no longer important whether anyone got to know that she had lived and what she had thought.

A cool night wind met them outside the hospital gate. A wind that was fragrant with the salty sea and new-mown hay. The wind would be at their backs and push them up across the steepest hills.

The rocking rhythm and the warmth of his body made her sleepy. She felt no pain or heavy sorrow, just a singular lightness.

She had never known such happiness.

The novel is set mainly in Bergen and takes place during the Napoleonic Wars, early in the 1800s, when famine and privation played havoc with the population. In those days leprosy was a common illness in Norway, and it increased in frequency throughout the 1800s. Johan Ernst Welhaven, father of the poet Johan Sebastian Cammermeyer Welhaven (1807–73), was in those days the pastor at St. Jørgen's Hospital in Bergen. There, leprosy patients from all of Vestland, the vast Western region of Norway, were interned for life. The majority came from the coastal towns and were torn away from their families to endure a bleak existence at the hospital. The illness took its course; many died, the majority became disfigured, and only a few recovered and could leave again.

Not until the 1840s did the hospital get its own doctor: Daniel C. Danielssen, who, together with Dr. C. W. Boeck, presented the first systematic description of this disease. Eventually they became so famous that medical researchers from the whole of Europe came to Bergen to study the illness. In 1873 Gerhard Armauer Hansen found the cause of leprosy, a rod-shaped bacillus. That was the first time a bacterium was proved to be the cause of a chronic disease among human beings. These discoveries belong among the greatest contributions that Norway has made to medicine throughout the ages. And the knowledge is of equal significance today in tropical countries, where leprosy still strikes many people. Even in Norway, the disease of leprosy existed until quite recently. In fact, there were patients at the hospital in Bergen right up to the 1960s.

St. Jørgens Hospital still stands unchanged from the way it was over two hundred years ago.

Professor Ole Didrik Lærum
Medical Director